AGATHA CHRISTIE

THE MURDER OF ROGER ACKROYD
BY BRUNO LACHARD
HARPER

HARPER
An imprint of HarperCollins*Publishers*
77-85 Fulham Palace Road
Hammersmith, London W6 8JB
www.harpercollins.co.uk

First published by HARPER 2007
1

Comic book edition published in France as *Le Meutre de Roger Ackroyd*

www.agathachristie.com

Adapted and illustrated by Bruno Lachard. Colour by Ongalro.
English edition edited by Steve Gove.

ISBN-13 978-0-00-725061-5
ISBN-10 0-00-725061-4

Printed and bound in Singapore by Imago.

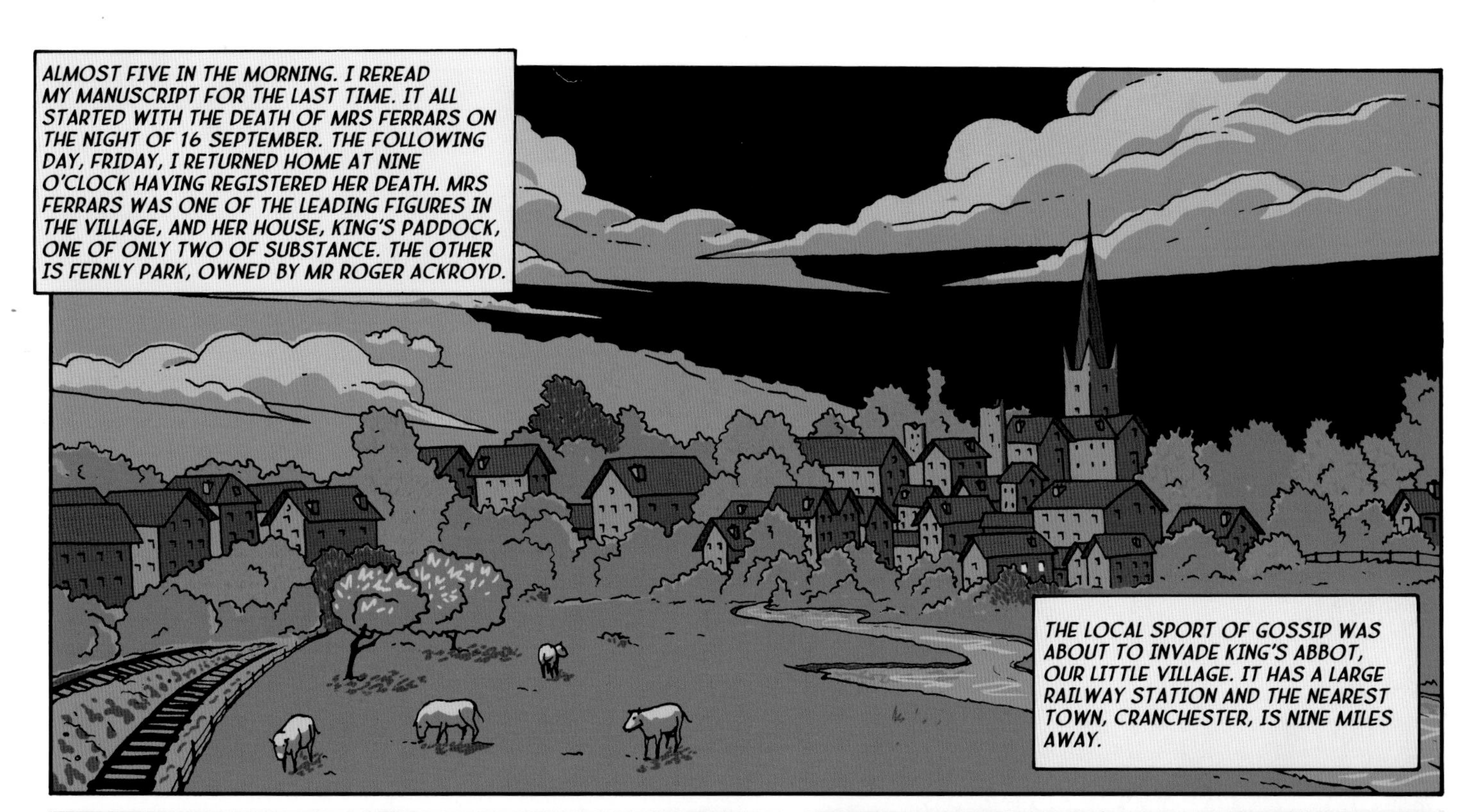
ALMOST FIVE IN THE MORNING. I REREAD MY MANUSCRIPT FOR THE LAST TIME. IT ALL STARTED WITH THE DEATH OF MRS FERRARS ON THE NIGHT OF 16 SEPTEMBER. THE FOLLOWING DAY, FRIDAY, I RETURNED HOME AT NINE O'CLOCK HAVING REGISTERED HER DEATH. MRS FERRARS WAS ONE OF THE LEADING FIGURES IN THE VILLAGE, AND HER HOUSE, KING'S PADDOCK, ONE OF ONLY TWO OF SUBSTANCE. THE OTHER IS FERNLY PARK, OWNED BY MR ROGER ACKROYD.
THE LOCAL SPORT OF GOSSIP WAS ABOUT TO INVADE KING'S ABBOT, OUR LITTLE VILLAGE. IT HAS A LARGE RAILWAY STATION AND THE NEAREST TOWN, CRANCHESTER, IS NINE MILES AWAY.

AS A DOCTOR, I AIM AT DISCRETION. MY SISTER, HOWEVER, IS A CHAMPION GOSSIP — A FACT WHICH CAUSES ME SOME DISQUIET.

AH YES, CAROLINE ... SHE INSISTS THAT MRS FERRARS KILLED HER HUSBAND, WHO DIED A YEAR AGO. OF COURSE, THE SYMPTOMS OF GASTRITIS AND ARSENIC POISONING ARE NOT UNALIKE...

THERE HAD BEEN RUMOURS THAT ACKROYD WOULD MARRY MRS FERRARS. ACKROYD'S STEPSON, THE CHARMING BUT FECKLESS RALPH PATON, WAS A CONSTANT SOURCE OF WORRY TO HIM.

WE WERE ALL FOND OF THE WAYWARD RALPH, WHOSE MOTHER HAD DIED SOME YEARS BEFORE.

ACKROYD'S WIDOWED SISTER-IN-LAW HAD RECENTLY RETURNED, PENNILESS, FROM CANADA WITH HER DAUGHTER, FLORA. MRS ACKROYD HAD SWIFTLY PUT ACKROYD'S HOUSEKEEPER IN HER PLACE, AND A MARRIAGE BETWEEN ACKROYD AND MRS FERRARS WOULD NOT HAVE BEEN TO HER ADVANTAGE.

I INFORMED CAROLINE THAT MRS FERRARS HAD DIED OF AN ACCIDENTAL OVERDOSE OF VERONAL. WHY WOULD SHE COMMIT SUICIDE?
Remorse!

She's had a haunted air in the last year. Ten to one she's left a letter.
She left no such thing!

Oh! So you enquired about that! I believe you think just as I do. But all will be revealed at the inquest.

There will be no need for an inquest, if I can declare myself satisfied that it was an accident...

And *are* you satisfied it was an accident?

VG 1966

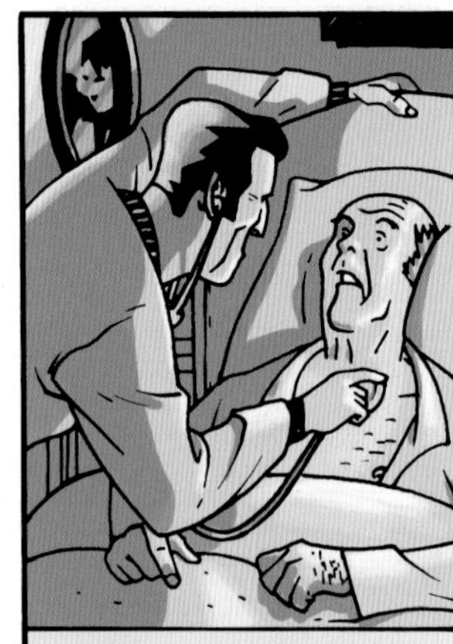
DURING MY ROUNDS THAT MORNING MY THOUGHTS CONSTANTLY RETURNED TO MRS FERRARS AND HER RELATIONSHIP WITH MR ACKROYD.

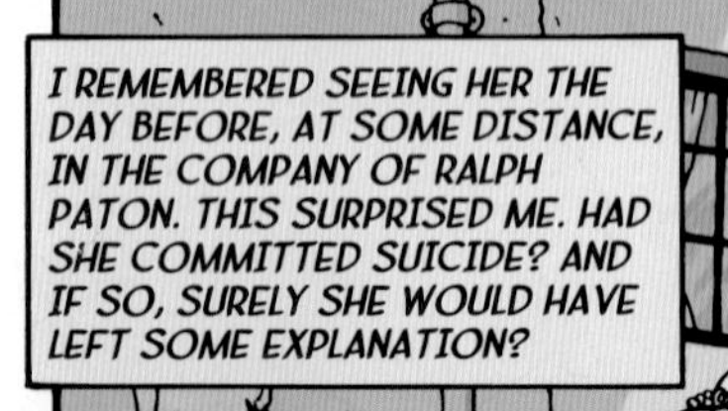
I REMEMBERED SEEING HER THE DAY BEFORE, AT SOME DISTANCE, IN THE COMPANY OF RALPH PATON. THIS SURPRISED ME. HAD SHE COMMITTED SUICIDE? AND IF SO, SURELY SHE WOULD HAVE LEFT SOME EXPLANATION?
Sheppard!

Ackroyd, have you heard...
Yes, it's a terrible business. Look, I must speak to you. Will you come to dine at Fernly tonight? Around 7 o'clock?

Yes, I can manage that. What's wrong? Is it Ralph?
Ralph? No, he's in London. It's about...
Damn! Here comes old Ganett. I must fly!

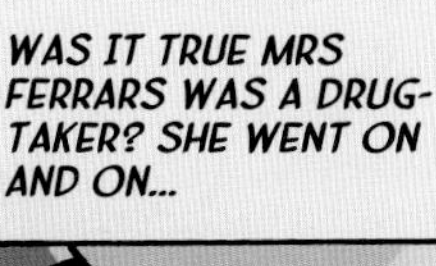
WAS IT TRUE MRS FERRARS WAS A DRUG-TAKER? SHE WENT ON AND ON...

BUT I HAVE LEARNED, AS A DOCTOR, TO REMAIN NON-COMMITTAL IN THE FACE OF SUCH GOSSIP.

HOWEVER, I WAS SURPRISED TO FIND THAT ACKROYD WAS UNAWARE OF RALPH PATON'S PRESENCE IN KING'S ABBOT.

Good morning, doctor.
Good morning, good morning...

HAVING SEEN WHAT I THOUGHT WAS THE MORNING'S LAST PATIENT, I FOUND ONE MORE AWAITING ME.
Goodbye. And have a good trip!

Ah, Miss Russell!
Good morning, doctor!

MISS RUSSELL CLAIMED TO BE SUFFERING PAINS IN HER KNEE

Thank you for this liniment, doctor. I don't believe in all these drugs.
Look at the cocaine habit! Suppose you were the slave to such a drug, is there any cure?

SUSPECTING THAT SHE SOUGHT INFORMATION ON MRS FERRARS, I LAID A TRAP FOR HER.
Now, Veronal, for example...

BUT SHE SHOWED NO INTEREST IN THE SUBJECT, AND TOOK HER LEAVE.
I SAW HER OUT IN TIME FOR LUNCH.

CAROLINE, OF COURSE, KNEW RALPH WAS IN KING'S ABBOT. HE HAD ARRIVED THE DAY BEFORE, BUT WAS STAYING AT THE THREE BOARS INSTEAD OF FERNLY PARK.
Ackroyd told me he was in London.

And last night he was out with a girl!
I didn't see her, but I'm sure it was Flora Ackroyd.

Flora?!

I'm sure they're secretly engaged. Ackroyd won't hear of it, so they have to meet this way.

UNCONVINCED ABOUT CAROLINE'S THEORY, I CHANGED THE SUBJECT. THE HOUSE NEXT DOOR, THE LARCHES, HAD JUST BEEN TAKEN BY A STRANGER.
CAROLINE HAD FAILED TO LEARN ANYTHING ABOUT OUR NEW NEIGHBOUR. WE KNEW ONLY THAT HIS NAME WAS PORROTT AND THAT HE GREW VEGETABLE MARROWS.

WITH HIS STRIKING APPEARANCE, HE SEEMED QUITE A CHARACTER...
...PROBABLY A RETIRED FOREIGN HAIRDRESSER!

ON THAT NOTE, I ESCAPED TO THE GARDEN TO TEND TO MY FLOWERS.

A thousand pardons, Monsieur. This morning my marrows, they enrage me!

... But it is not with me a habit!
A man may retire, may toil to attain leisure, and then find himself yearning for his old occupations...

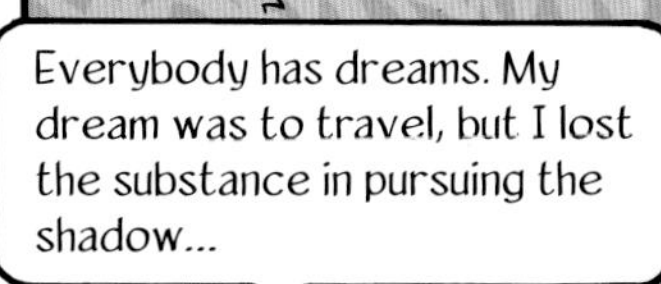

Everybody has dreams. My dream was to travel, but I lost the substance in pursuing the shadow...
I lost a considerable legacy through rash investments.
I comprehend, Monsieur. My daily labour was the study of human nature.

CLEARLY A RETIRED HAIRDRESSER! HE TOLD ME OF HIS DEAR FRIEND HASTINGS, NOW IN THE ARGENTINE.

And you say you know Ralph Paton?
I knew Mr Ackroyd in London, and he has often spoken to me about Ralph. And so he is engaged to the charming Miss Flora...

But I believe he brought some pressure to bear. That is never wise.

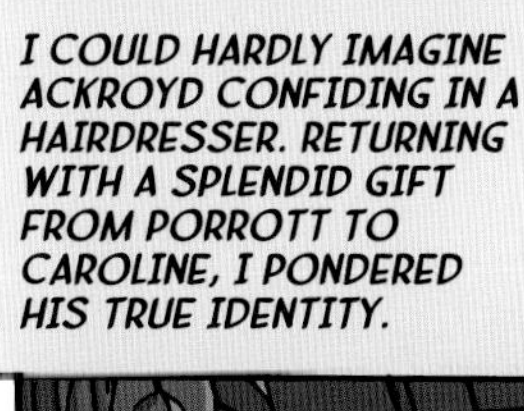
I COULD HARDLY IMAGINE ACKROYD CONFIDING IN A HAIRDRESSER. RETURNING WITH A SPLENDID GIFT FROM PORROTT TO CAROLINE, I PONDERED HIS TRUE IDENTITY.

I met Mr Ackroyd in the village. He told me that Ralph and Flora are engaged!
I know that too. Porrott, our new neighbour, gave me the news.

Oh... I told Mr Ackroyd that Ralph was staying at the Three Boars.
That was hardly a wise thing to do!

Nonsense. Mr Ackroyd was very grateful to me.
He went straight there, but I doubt that he found Ralph there.

I went for a walk in the woods, and I'm sure I heard Ralph's voice...

We need the money, my dear.
I shall be rich once he's dead. He's as mean as they come, but he's rolling in money. I don't want him changing his will. Leave it all to me...!

CAROLINE WAS SURE THE YOUNG GIRL MUST HAVE BEEN FLORA. BUT IF SHE AND RALPH WERE ENGAGED, THE CONVERSATION MADE NO SENSE.
SO I DECIDED TO MAKE MY WAY TO THE THREE BOARS.

Things haven't been going well for me, doctor. I'm in the devil of a mess. It's my confounded stepfather...
Perhaps I can help...?

Good of you, doctor. But I can't let you in on this.
I've got to play a lone hand.

Yes, a lone hand...

THAT EVENING I WENT TO FERNLY PARK AS ARRANGED. I WAS GREETED BY THE BUTLER, PARKER, AND THE SECRETARY, RAYMOND.
Good evening, sir.
Good evening, doctor.

Coming to dine? Or is this a professional call?
Please go into the drawing room. I must just take these papers to Mr Ackroyd. I'll tell him you're here.

BANG!

Oh, I'm sorry, Dr Sheppard!

I only came in to make sure the flowers were fresh.
Do excuse me, Miss Russell. How's the knee?

Much the same, thank you — I didn't know you would be dining tonight.

MISS RUSSELL WAS ACTING RATHER STRANGELY...

BANG!
I SOON DISCOVERED WHERE THE NOISE I HAD HEARD MUST HAVE COME FROM.

Dr Sheppard, have you been looking at King Charles the First's shoes?
Good evening, Miss Flora.

You haven't congratulated me yet. Ralph and I have been engaged for a month, but it was only announced yesterday.
I hope you'll be very happy, my dear.

The dear young things, they'll make a lovely couple — he so dark and she so fair!

Doctor, you are such an old friend of Roger's. Could you ... sound him out on the matter of Flora's settlement?
Roger is so close — and a little odd about money.

I WAS SAVED FROM THIS LINE OF ENQUIRY BY THE ENTRY OF MAJOR BLUNT, A BIG GAME HUNTER AND AN OLD FRIEND OF ACKROYD'S.

I HAVE HEARD BLUNT DESCRIBED AS A WOMAN-HATER, BUT HE WENT TO FLORA'S SIDE WITH ALACRITY.
Do tell me about these African objects.

THAT EVENING ACKROYD ATE NEXT TO NOTHING. HE SEEMED PREOCCUPIED.
AFTER DINNER HE LED ME OFF TO HIS STUDY.

Coffee, sir?
Doctor, that pain after eating has returned lately...
Parker, perhaps you would fetch my bag?

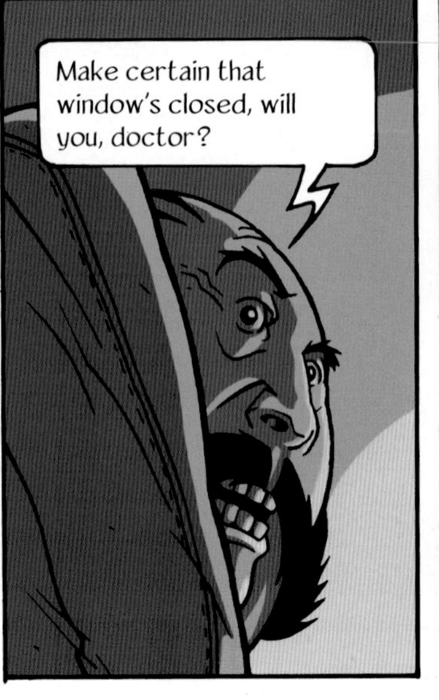
Make certain that window's closed, will you, doctor?

Is it fully secured?
Yes, it's shut. Thank you, Parker.

It's all right, Sheppard. I don't need a tablet. But servants are so curious. Is the door closed?
Yes. No one can overhear. Don't be uneasy.

Sheppard, I'm in hell. This business of Ralph's is the last straw. And...
...there's the other matter.
Sheppard, you treated Ashley Ferrars, didn't you?

Did you ever suspect — that he was poisoned?
Well, I had no such suspicion at the time! But since then—

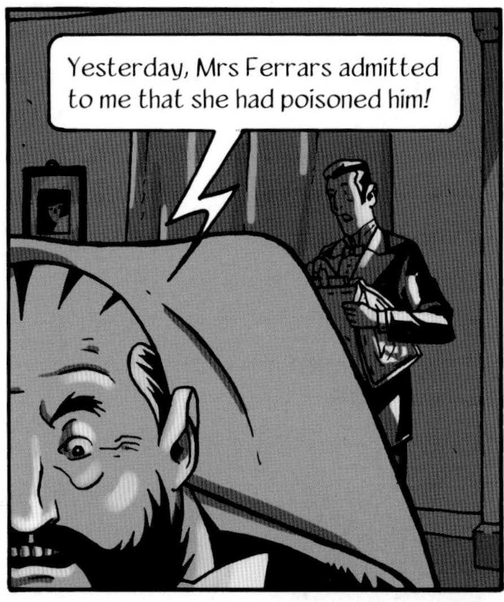
Yesterday, Mrs Ferrars admitted to me that she had poisoned him!

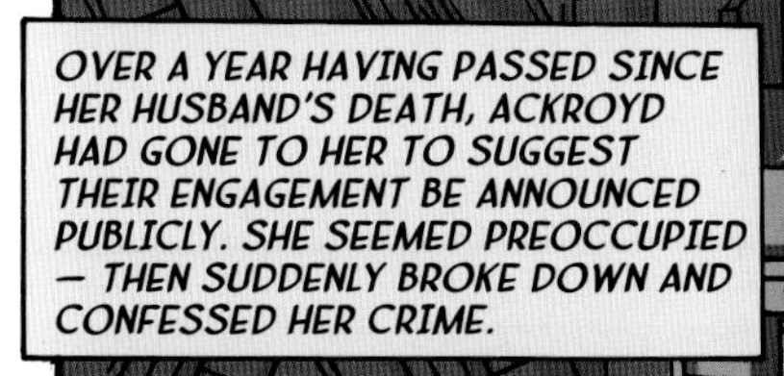
OVER A YEAR HAVING PASSED SINCE HER HUSBAND'S DEATH, ACKROYD HAD GONE TO HER TO SUGGEST THEIR ENGAGEMENT BE ANNOUNCED PUBLICLY. SHE SEEMED PREOCCUPIED — THEN SUDDENLY BROKE DOWN AND CONFESSED HER CRIME.

SHE HAD MURDERED HER HUSBAND FOR ACKROYD'S SAKE. BUT SOMEONE HAD KNOWN ABOUT IT AND WAS BLACKMAILING HER.

I RECALLED THE DISCUSSION BETWEEN RALPH AND MRS FERRARS.

AN ABSURD THOUGHT CROSSED MY MIND. SURELY NOT RALPH? HE HAD SEEMED SO GENUINE.

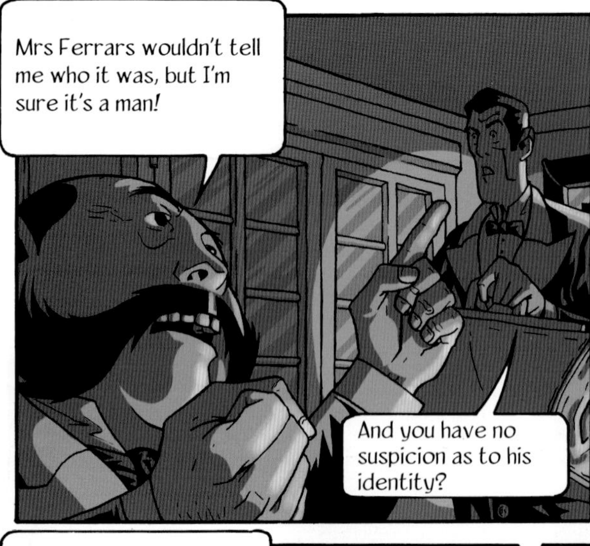
Mrs Ferrars wouldn't tell me who it was, but I'm sure it's a man!
And you have no suspicion as to his identity?

Something she said made me think it might be a member of my household...
But that's impossible...!

She implored me to wait for 24 hours before taking any action.
My God, Sheppard, it never entered my head that she'd kill herself!

The blackmailer must pay for this!!!
But think of the consequences ... the publicity!

I'm convinced she left me a message of some kind.
She certainly didn't leave a letter.

Sir, the evening post.

It's her handwriting!

I've had a queer feeling this evening of being spied on. Are you sure the window's shut?
Quite sure.

CLICK...

10,

"A life calls for a life ... I leave to you the punishment of my blackmailer. I have no near relations, so do not fear publicity..." There's more —

Forgive me, Sheppard, but I must read this alone...
No, read it now. I mean, please read it while I am here.

BUT ACKROYD WAS ADAMANT. THE LETTER HAD BEEN BROUGHT TO HIM AT TWENTY MINUTES TO NINE. WHEN I LEFT TEN MINUTES LATER, IT WAS STILL UNREAD.

I FOUND PARKER CLOSE BY. HAD HE BEEN LISTENING AT THE DOOR? INFORMING HIM THAT ACKROYD WAS NOT TO BE DISTURBED, I LEFT THE HOUSE.

This the way to Fernly Park, mister?
Through here.

THE CLOCK STRUCK NINE.
THE STRANGER'S VOICE REMINDED ME OF SOMEONE BUT I COULD NOT BRING TO MIND WHO IT WAS.

ARRIVING HOME TEN MINUTES LATER, I INVENTED AN ACCOUNT OF THE EVENING TO SATISFY CAROLINE. BUT I SUSPECTED THAT SHE SAW THROUGH THE DECEPTION.

Good night, James.
TRING!

TRING!

11,

Hello?
What! How...?

I'll come at once!

It's Parker. He says Ackroyd has been murdered!

TING TING TING

Where is Mr Ackroyd?
And have you contacted the police?!

The police, sir?

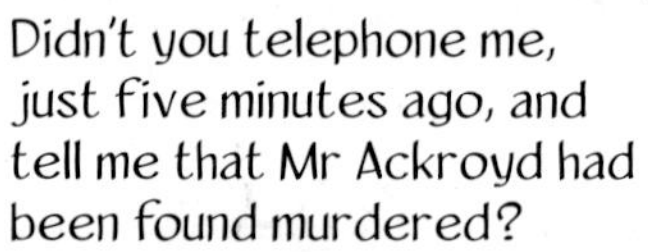
Didn't you telephone me, just five minutes ago, and tell me that Mr Ackroyd had been found murdered?

No indeed, sir. I did no such thing.

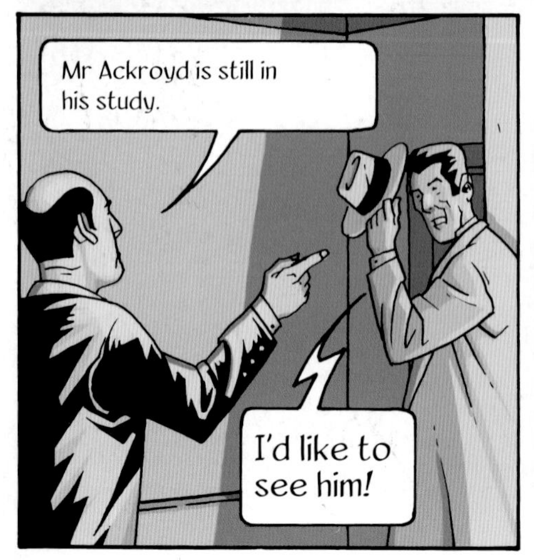
Mr Ackroyd is still in his study.
I'd like to see him!

BANG! BANG!!

Ackroyd! Ackroyd!
The key is in the lock. He must have locked himself in and fallen asleep.

Close the door to the hallway.
I shan't be satisfied unless I hear from his own lips that he's all right.
We must break down the door!

CRACK!!!

This is horrible!
Don't touch the weapon! You must ring the police. And then tell Mr Raymond and Major Blunt.

Mr Raymond! Someone's murdered Mr Ackroyd!

My God!

You mustn't touch anything. The police must see him exactly as he is now.

There was nothing important here. Nothing's missing.

Look, there are some letters on the floor.
BUT MRS FERRARS' LETTER HAD DISAPPEARED. I WAS ABOUT TO SPEAK WHEN...

13,

Good evening, gentlemen. Inspector Davis. The butler says it's murder. No chance of a mistake, doctor?
I hope nobody's touched the body. Who discovered it?
I EXPLAINED THE CIRCUMSTANCES, ADDING THAT I ESTIMATED ACKROYD TO HAVE BEEN DEAD FOR AT LEAST HALF AN HOUR.

Did you recognize Parker's voice, doctor?
No, I can't say I did.
I've not used the telephone this evening. The others will testify to that.

The door was locked from inside, you say? What about the window?
I closed and bolted it myself, at Ackroyd's request.

Look!

Nothing missing? The intruder stabbed Ackroyd, then lost his nerve and made off without taking anything.

Any suspicious strangers been hanging about?

I TOLD HIM ABOUT MY ENCOUNTER WITH THE STRANGER AT THE GATES TO FERNLY PARK.

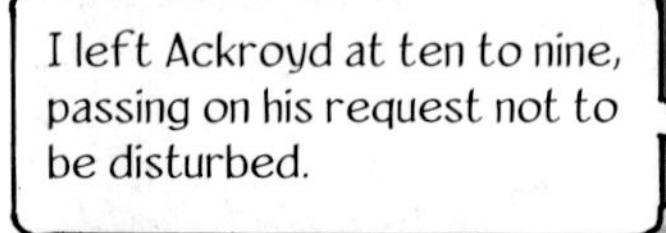
I left Ackroyd at ten to nine, passing on his request not to be disturbed.

I heard his voice at half past nine and assumed he was talking to you, doctor. I wonder who it was, then? It seemed an odd conversation...

The calls on my funds have been so frequent of late... It is impossible for me to accede to your request.

I was at home with my sister by a quarter past nine.
And I never saw Ackroyd after dinner.

A demand for money ... and no one was admitted to the house this evening?
So Ackroyd opened the door to the stranger himself.

I saw Miss Flora coming out of the study at a quarter to ten when I was taking a whisky to Mr Ackroyd. I'd forgotten about the order not to disturb him.
Hmm, I must see Miss Ackroyd at once. But please, no one's to tell her what's happened.

This staircase only leads to Mr Ackroyd's bedroom. It's separate from the rest of the house.
Lock the door to the main hall so no one can go in that room.

Miss Ackroyd, I'm afraid there's been a burglary. Did you see your uncle around a quarter to ten?

Yes. He was alone. Dr Sheppard had gone by then. What has been stolen?
Did you notice whether the window was closed?

I can't say. The curtains were drawn. My uncle said good night and asked me to ensure he wasn't disturbed.
Won't you tell me what's been stolen?

I'm sorry, Miss Ackroyd. Your uncle has been murdered.

When?
When?!

Shortly after you left him, I'm afraid to say.

BLUNT AND I CARRIED HER TO HER BEDROOM. THEN I CAME DOWNSTAIRS AGAIN.

15,
Can you tell us anything more about that stranger you saw, Dr Sheppard?
I'm sorry, it was very dark. But his voice seemed familiar to me.
Parker's come up with some story about blackmail...

APPARENTLY PARKER HAD BEEN LISTENING AT THE DOOR. SO I INFORMED THE INSPECTOR THAT MRS FERRARS HAD INDEED BEEN BLACKMAILED.

The letter, accusing a member of Ackroyd's staff, disappeared ... it looked bad for Parker.
But if Ackroyd believed it was Parker, he would have confronted him immediately.

Yes ... but someone was here at half past nine ... then Miss Ackroyd came. He wouldn't have finished the letter before ten.
So Parker killed him, then made the telephone call. But then he panicked and tried to deny it.

Let's look at the dagger ... there are fingerprints on it!
The murderer must be right-handed. Ackroyd would have died instantly, without even seeing his assailant.

Butlers can creep about as quietly as cats!
I want to see if Raymond or Blunt can tell us anything about this dagger.

I gave Ackroyd that dagger. It comes from Tunis. He used to keep it in the display case in the drawing room.
What?!

When I arrived for dinner last night, I heard someone closing the display case in the drawing room.
RELUCTANTLY, I EXPLAINED EVERYTHING TO THE INSPECTOR. WHEN I TOLD HIM I WAS UNABLE TO REMEMBER WHETHER THE DAGGER HAD BEEN INSIDE THE CASE, HE SUMMONED MISS RUSSELL.

The lid of the case was open, so I shut it. But I can't say whether the dagger was still inside.
Were the French windows open? If so, anyone could have taken the dagger.

RAYMOND HANDED ME A VISITING CARD AND TOOK ANOTHER HIMSELF. ONCE WE HAD HANDLED THEM, HE OFFERED THEM TO THE INSPECTOR.
Fingerprints, inspector. Number One from Dr Sheppard, Number Two from my humble self. One from Major Blunt will soon be forthcoming.

WHEN I RETURNED HOME, NATURALLY CAROLINE WAS WAITING FOR ME. I SAID NOTHING OF BLACKMAIL, BUT TOLD HER OF THE MURDER AND THE SUSPICIONS WEIGHING ON PARKER.
Parker indeed! That inspector must be a perfect fool!

NEXT DAY, ON RETURNING FROM MY ROUND, I FOUND FLORA IN THE SITTING ROOM.
Dr Sheppard, I want you to come to The Larches with me.

Why? To see Porrott, the retired hairdresser?
What? He's Hercule Poirot, the private detective. He's come here to live incognito.

MISS FLORA HAD LITTLE CONFIDENCE IN INSPECTOR DAVIS. SO SHE THOUGHT THAT I — AS THE DOCTOR, AND HAVING FOUND THE BODY — WOULD BE ABLE TO PERSUADE POIROT TO HELP.

Are you sure it's the truth you want to know?
Why, you're afraid! The servants at the Three Boars told me you went there last night asking for Ralph. But he'd gone out at nine ... and never came back!

Leaving his luggage behind?!
There must be some explanation.

Don't worry. Davis is on Parker's track.
Parker!

But it's Inspector Raglan from Cranchester who is conducting the investigation now. And he suspects Ralph!
And yes, doctor, I at least do want to know the truth.

CAROLINE, TOO, WAS SURE OF RALPH'S INNOCENCE: "SUCH A DEAR BOY, WITH THE NICEST MANNERS!" SO I WENT WITH FLORA TO THE LARCHES.
Monsieur le docteur ... Mademoiselle.

Monsieur Poirot, perhaps you have heard about last night's tragic events? Miss Ackroyd would like you to investigate.
I see. You must understand, if I undertake this case I shall go through with it to the very end!

Monsieur Poirot, I want the truth. All the truth!
WITH A TWINKLE IN HIS EYE, POIROT DECLINED ANY SUGGESTION OF PAYMENT. I BEGAN TO RECOUNT THE DETAILS OF THE CASE...

As possibly the only one, apart from Ackroyd himself, to know that Ralph was at the Three Boars, I thought I should tell him of his uncle's death.
It was not to — shall we say — reassure yourself that the *jeune homme* was in his room?

Not at all!
No matter. Ralph Paton's disappearance may admit of a perfectly simple explanation.

POIROT SUGGESTED THAT HE AND I SHOULD VISIT THE LOCAL POLICE. FLORA, MEANWHILE, WAS TO RETURN HOME.
POIROT ADOPTED AN ATTITUDE OF PERFECT HUMILITY BEFORE THE POLICE OFFICERS.

WE SET OFF AT ONCE FOR FERNLY, ACCOMPANIED BY INSPECTORS DAVIS AND RAGLAN, AS WELL AS THE CHIEF INSPECTOR, COLONEL MELROSE.

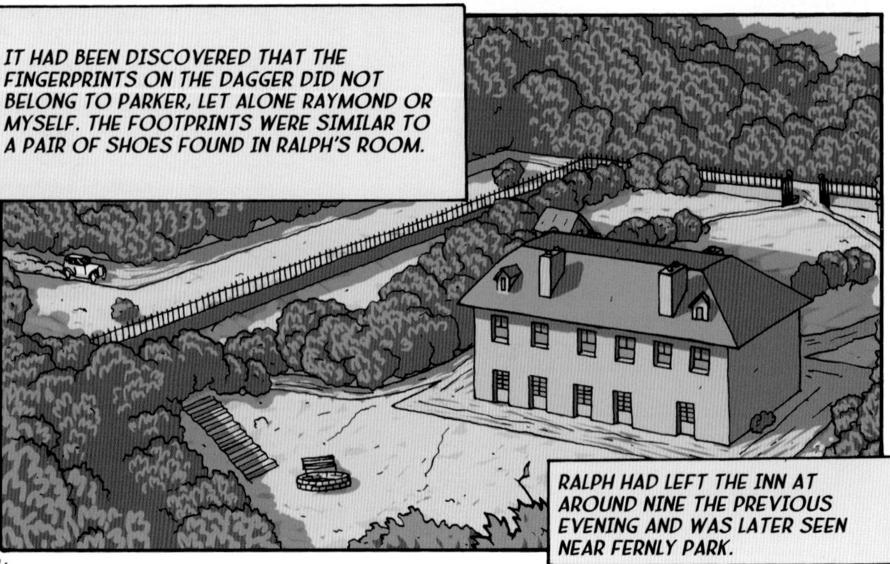
IT HAD BEEN DISCOVERED THAT THE FINGERPRINTS ON THE DAGGER DID NOT BELONG TO PARKER, LET ALONE RAYMOND OR MYSELF. THE FOOTPRINTS WERE SIMILAR TO A PAIR OF SHOES FOUND IN RALPH'S ROOM.
RALPH HAD LEFT THE INN AT AROUND NINE THE PREVIOUS EVENING AND WAS LATER SEEN NEAR FERNLY PARK.

RAGLAN EXPLORED THE TERRACE WHILE POIROT RECONSTRUCTED THE SCENE IN THE STUDY WHEN THE BODY WAS FOUND.
The light, it was on? And the envelope was on the little table. The dagger was like this?
The hilt of the dagger was then visible from the door. You and Parker saw it at once?

But let us proceed with method. You observed the body, doctor; Parker did the room...

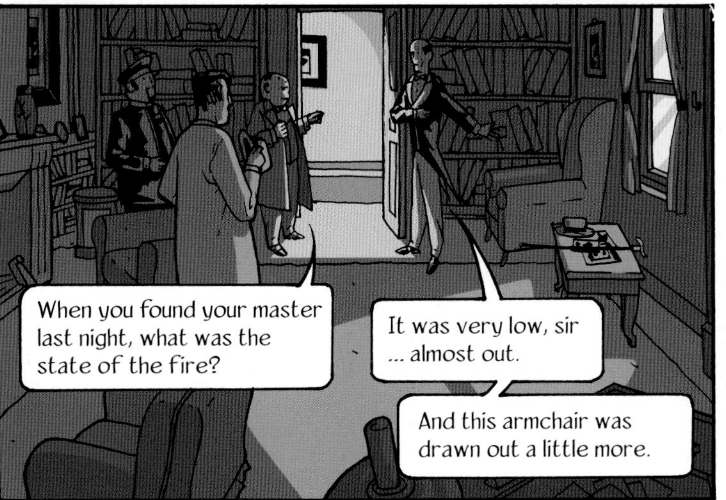
When you found your master last night, what was the state of the fire?
It was very low, sir ... almost out.
And this armchair was drawn out a little more.

Like this.
C'est curieux. Who pushed it back, I wonder?

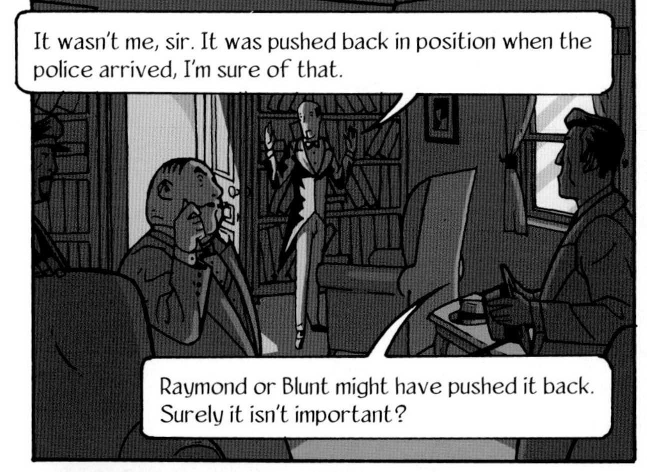
It wasn't me, sir. It was pushed back in position when the police arrived, I'm sure of that.
Raymond or Blunt might have pushed it back. Surely it isn't important?

It is completely unimportant. That is why it is interesting.

Do you think Parker is telling the truth?
But in such a case, everyone has something to hide. You, for instance, about Ralph Paton...

The night was cold, the fire low. Ackroyd must have opened the window only to admit someone ... a person he know well.

Did your stranger enter through the window at around a quarter to ten to kill Ackroyd?

Your telephone call last night, doctor ... it came from the station. And less than five minutes before the express left for Liverpool!

KING'S ABBOT STATION IS AN IMPORTANT JUNCTION FROM WHICH MANY PASSENGERS TAKE THE EXPRESS TO THE NORTH.

When we know the reason for that telephone call, we shall know everything!
How long would the stranger need to get from the gate to this window, doctor?

Five minutes at most. Two or three, if he took the path on the right to the gate.

But to do that he must have been familiar with his surroundings. Perhaps Parker or Raymond will know of any strangers visiting Fernly in the recent past?

A dictaphone salesman called last Wednesday, but Mr Ackroyd purchased nothing from him. He bore no resemblance to Dr Sheppard's stranger. And as for the armchair — no, I didn't move it.

Mr Hammond, the family solicitor, is here.

This case should be quite straightforward. As long as we use method.
Method, yes ... and also the little grey cells!

The cells?
The little grey cells of the brain. We all use them ... to a greater or lesser degree!

We know that Flora Ackroyd was the last to see her uncle alive, at a quarter to ten.

If you say so.

Now, according to the doctor, Ackroyd died at around ten o'clock. I've asked everyone what they were doing between nine forty-five and ten.

MAJOR BLUNT AND RAYMOND WERE IN THE BILLIARD ROOM WITH MRS ACKROYD.

SHE WENT TO BED AT NINE FIFTY-FIVE AND THEY ACCOMPANIED HER TO THE STAIRCASE.

MISS FLORA WENT STRAIGHT UPSTAIRS FROM HER UNCLE'S ROOM. THIS WAS CONFIRMED BY PARKER AND MISS ELSIE DALE.

PARKER THEN SPOKE TO MISS RUSSELL IN THE PANTRY AT AROUND NINE FORTY-SEVEN.

BEFORE THAT MISS RUSSELL SPOKE TO ELSIE DALE UPSTAIRS AT NINE FORTY-SIX.

THE PARLOURMAID, URSULA BOURNE, WAS IN HER ROOM UNTIL NINE FIFTY-FIVE. THEN SHE WENT TO THE SERVANTS' HALL.

AT THIS TIME THE THIRD MAID, THE COOK AND THE KITCHENMAID ALL STAYED IN THE SERVANTS' HALL...

...WHILE ELSIE DALE REMAINED UPSTAIRS IN THE BEDROOM. MISS RUSSELL SAW HER THERE.

Their alibis rule most of them out. And they all seem honest enough. Except Parker — something fishy about him.
Parker is not the murderer!

Now, the keeper of the Lodge saw Ralph Paton going towards the house at nine twenty-five.
At half past nine someone asked Ackroyd for money.

Having been refused, Paton left through the window, took the dagger from the drawing room and returned to the study.

Then...!
Next, he made for the station and rang up from there.
But why?

Murderers sometimes do funny things. And then there are Ralph Paton's footprints near the window — and here!
A foolish criminal, to leave so much evidence! And a great many people wear shoes similar to Ralph's.

Besides, there are women's footprints too.
There would be. It's a regular short cut to the house.

You are still by my side, doctor? You remind me of my friend Hastings!

What have you found?

A feather...

...and a scrap of starched linen.

Not a handkerchief. A good washerwoman does not starch a handkerchief!

Tell me, who inherits this fine property of Fernly Park?
Good heavens, I hadn't thought of that! I wish I had...

I wonder what you mean by that?
As you say, Poirot, everyone has something to hide.
And Hercule Poirot discovers it all!

BELOW US WE SAW FLORA, ALMOST DANCING ALONG THE PATH. THEN BLUNT APPEARED.

THEY HADN'T NOTICED US. POIROT MADE ME STAY SILENT.

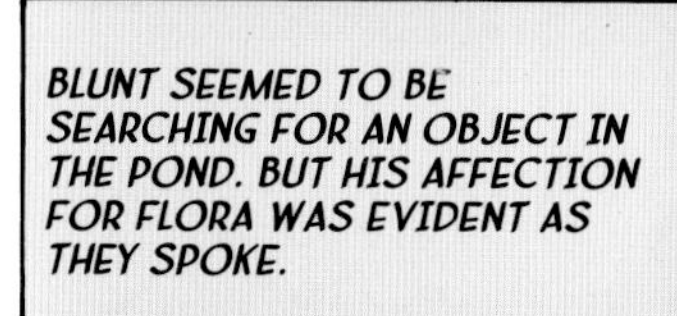
BLUNT SEEMED TO BE SEARCHING FOR AN OBJECT IN THE POND. BUT HIS AFFECTION FOR FLORA WAS EVIDENT AS THEY SPOKE.

FLORA WAS TELLING HIM ABOUT HER INHERITANCE. WITH TWENTY THOUSAND POUNDS, SHE SAID, THERE NEED BE NO MORE DEBTS, NO MORE LIES. SHE EXPRESSED HER CERTAINTY THAT WITH POIROT'S HELP, RALPH WOULD BE SAVED.

Mademoiselle, please spare my blushes. I must beg your pardon.

Major Blunt, I'm delighted to make your acquaintance.
I am also in need of some information that perhaps you can give me.

AFTER DINNER BLUNT HAD BEEN OUT ON THE TERRACE, WHERE AT HALF PAST NINE HE HAD HEARD ACKROYD SPEAKING WITH SOMEONE. BUT HE HAD NOT MOVED THE ARMCHAIR.

Surely you could not hear him from the terrace?

Actually, I went as far as the corner of the house. I thought I saw a woman in white disappearing into the bushes.

Something glitters in this pond... Mademoiselle, when you were in the drawing room with Dr Sheppard, was the dagger in the display case?
I'm perfectly certain it wasn't, but Raglan doesn't believe me. He thinks I'm saying so to shield Ralph.

And aren't you?
You too, Dr Sheppard! It's too bad!

I couldn't reach this object... Never mind. Shall we go to lunch?

They will make a pretty couple. Miss Ackroyd with her hair so golden, and the dark, handsome Ralph Paton!
You've made yourself muddy for nothing.

Do you tell your patients absolutely everything, doctor? Or your sister? Nor does Hercule Poirot. *Mon ami*, I am never ridiculous in vain!

"From R, 13th March."

Mr Hammond is lunching with us.
This is Monsieur Poirot, mother. He is to find out who killed Uncle.

But surely it must have been an accident? Roger was so fond of such curious objects. His hand must have slipped...

A POLITE SILENCE GREETED MRS ACKROYD'S THEORY. IT WAS BROKEN WHEN POIROT ADDRESSED MR HAMMOND.

Miss Ackroyd has asked me to investigate the death of her uncle.
I cannot believe Ralph Paton to be involved in this crime. The fact that he was in need of money proves nothing!

The terms of the will are simple. A thousand pounds to Miss Russell, five hundred to Mr Raymond, twenty thousand for Miss Flora and the income from ten thousand pounds to Mrs Ackroyd. The rest — including this property — goes to Ralph Paton.
Mr Hammond!

Would you be able to assist me?
POIROT WISHED ME TO QUESTION MAJOR BLUNT DISCREETLY ABOUT MRS FERRARS AND HER HUSBAND.

BLUNT TOLD ME OF THE CHANGE HE HAD SEEN IN MRS FERRARS SINCE HER HUSBAND'S DEATH. HE ALSO ADMITTED HAVING LOST MONEY THROUGH A FOOLISH INVESTMENT. I SYMPATHIZED, REVEALING MY OWN SIMILAR ERROR.

CERTAIN THAT BLUNT WAS ABOVE SUSPICION, I TOOK MY LEAVE AND REPORTED TO POIROT.
AFTER LUNCH, MRS ACKROYD TOOK ME TO ONE SIDE...

That twenty thousand pounds should have been left to me — not Flora. After all, I am her mother, as well as the widow of Roger's brother. But Roger was always rather ... mean. And to leave a thousand pounds to that Miss Russell!
Something odd about her, I've always said. But Roger admired her. She did her best to marry him, you know, but I soon put a stop to that. She always hated me...

Madam, I wanted to let you know that the inquest is to be held this Monday.

The inquest? But surely Dr Sheppard can deal with everything? If the death was an accident...
He was murdered, Mrs Ackroyd!

But if there's an inquest... Shall I have to answer questions, and all that?
I HAD NO SYMPATHY FOR WHAT I THOUGHT WAS HER SILLY SQUEAMISHNESS.

25,

And if you need ready money, Mr Ackroyd cashed a cheque for a hundred pounds yesterday. The money is still in his bedroom.
I think we ought to make sure the money is there before I leave.

So Ackroyd kept his cash in an old box, without a lock?
Mr Ackroyd trusted his servants implicitly.

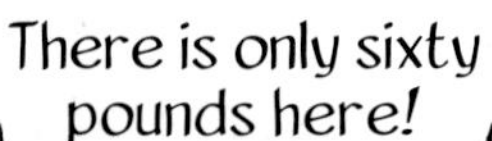

There is only sixty pounds here!

Which of the servants would have come into this room yesterday evening?
There's Elsie, the housemaid, but she's very trustworthy. *Oh*, and Ursula Bourne. She gave notice to Miss Russell yesterday...

Elsie Dale could never have have done such a thing...
...and Ursula Bourne is an excellent worker too. But Mr Ackroyd found fault with her yesterday. He was annoyed, and she gave her notice.

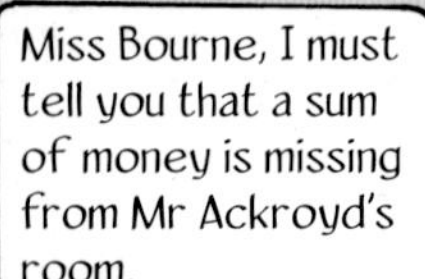

Miss Bourne, I must tell you that a sum of money is missing from Mr Ackroyd's room.

If you think I'm a thief, you can search my suitcases!
I moved some papers on Mr Ackroyd's desk yesterday. He spoke to me about it for half an hour, and at the end of it he dismissed me.

How long has Ursula been here? Does she have any references?
There's her letter of recommendation. It's from Mrs Richard Folliott of Marby Grange

As for Parker, he's a bit fishy! But he's got an alibi for the whole evening.
Anyway, it's likely that Mr Ackroyd paid the money to someone himself.

Raymond told us that there were no papers of importance on Ackroyd's desk.
And did you notice, my friend, that the only person whose alibi had no confirmation is Ursula Bourne?
But surely you don't think she killed Ackroyd? And the blackmailer is a man...

Is the blackmailer a man, doctor?
Mrs Ferrars mentioned a person in her letter — but Ackroyd and I took it for granted that it was a man.

So, it's possible... but...

I must have method!
Would it be possible for you to go to Marby tomorrow? To see Mrs Folliott and find out about Ursula Bourne?

ARRIVING AT MARBY THE NEXT DAY I WONDERED WHY POIROT HAD SENT ME ON THIS MISSION. MRS FOLLIOTT RECEIVED ME WITH LITTLE WARMTH...
GROWING ANGRY, SHE FLUNG UP HER HEAD IN A GESTURE THAT SEEMED VAGUELY FAMILIAR.

AS A DOCTOR, I CAN USUALLY TELL WHEN PEOPLE ARE LYING. PLAINLY SHE DID NOT WISH TO REVEAL THE MYSTERY SURROUNDING URSULA BOURNE. TAKING MY LEAVE, I WENT TO SEE MY PATIENTS.

ONCE HOME, I FOUND CAROLINE IN A MOOD OF SUPPRESSED EXULTATION...
I've had a very interesting afternoon with Monsieur Poirot. He told me a lot about himself and his cases. Did you know he has solved mysteries for royalty?

I was able to set him straight on some points concerning the murder. Even though his little grey cells, he says, are of the finest quality.
Modesty is certainly not his middle name!
HOW CLEVER OF POIROT! HE UNDERSTOOD PRECISELY HOW TO APPEAL TO AN ELDERLY LADY LIVING IN A SMALL VILLAGE.

Monsieur Poirot thinks it very important that Ralph should be found as soon as possible.
I was surprised to find that you hadn't told him about my seeing Ralph.

I took very good care not to!
The truth can't hurt him. Very likely he was with the same girl the night of the murder. She's his alibi, but he won't come forward in case she gets into trouble.

You read too many novels!
He also asked me which patients you saw that morning in your surgery.

There was old Mrs Bennett, the farmhand, Dolly Grice, that American steward from the liner, old George Evans...
...and Miss Russell! There's something odd about her...

She no more had a bad knee than you or I! She was after something else, and Monsieur Poirot wants to know what it was.
I REMEMBERED SHE HAD QUESTIONED ME ABOUT POISONS. BUT ACKROYD HAD NOT BEEN POISONED...

ON MONDAY I APPEARED AT THE INQUEST. RALPH PATON'S DESCRIPTION HAD BEEN CIRCULATED TO EVERY STATION AND PORT. HE HAD NO LUGGAGE AND NO MONEY. HOW COULD HE ESCAPE DETECTION?
Why has Ralph Paton not come forward? He telephoned the doctor three minutes before the Liverpool express left.

Perhaps the message was intended to throw the police off the scent? But once we know why that call was made, we will know the name of the murderer!
We've better clues than that. The fingerprints on the dagger for instance. The don't belong to anyone in the house, which leaves Ralph Paton and the stranger at the gate as the only suspects.

Nor do they belong to Mr Ackroyd?

You're not suggesting suicide?
Ah! No. Perhaps the murderer wore gloves? After striking, he closed the victim's hand round the dagger? Thus he adds confusion to the case.

Well, I'll look into it.

Another time, I must be more careful of the inspector's self-esteem!

What do you say to a little family reunion?

HALF AN HOUR LATER WE WERE ALL GATHERED AT FERNLY.
Mademoiselle Flora, as Ralph's fiancée, I beg you earnestly to persuade him to come forward.
I swear to you, I have no idea where Ralph is!

Ralph's absence is most peculiar, as though there were something more to it... Flora dear, it was very fortunate that your engagement was never formally announced.
Not that I think Ralph was the murderer. But his behaviour can be erratic...

Mother!
Come now, Madame!

What would happen to Roger's estate if Ralph were guilty?
My engagement to Ralph will be announced officially tomorrow!

Flora!
I must stand by Ralph. I'm not disloyal to my friends!

She's doing the right thing. I'll stand by her through thick and thin.
Mademoiselle, please do not misunderstand me. But I ask you to postpone your announcement for one or two days. In Ralph's interest as well as yours, I ask you not to hamper my investigation!

All right — I will do what you say.

In all probability this wil be my last case, and Hercule Poirot has no wish to end with a failure, in spite of you all!
Yes, every one of you is concealing something from me. But you will speak out in the end. Come now, the truth — the whole truth.

Will no one speak? *C'est dommage!*

I WENT TO SEE POIROT THAT EVENING. OVER DRINKS, HE ASKED WHY I HAD NOT INFORMED HIM OF RALPH'S MEETING IN THE WOODS.
I SUGGESTED THAT HE HAD BEEN GIVING CAROLINE A SWELLED HEAD. HE REPLIED THAT HE ALWAYS LIKED TO EMPLOY THE EXPERT. BUT ON THE SUBJECT OF MISS RUSSELL, HE WOULD SAY LITTLE.
30,

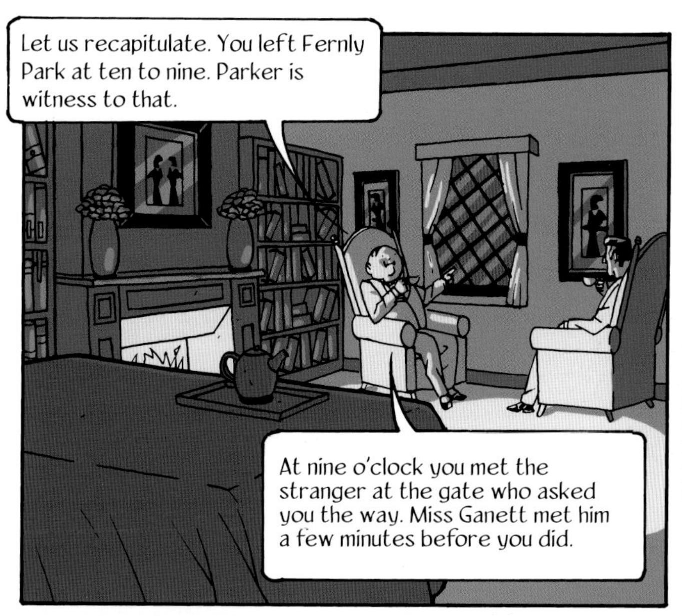
Let us recapitulate. You left Fernly Park at ten to nine. Parker is witness to that.
At nine o'clock you met the stranger at the gate who asked you the way. Miss Ganett met him a few minutes before you did.

He had a drink at the Three Boars, where the barmaid says he spoke with a slight American accent.
You remember the feather? In North America, drug addicts use such an item to sniff heroin.

He was unfamiliar with the neighbourhood, therefore, and he made no secret of his visit to Fernly Park.
What attracted your attention to the outhouse?

No one came to the door of Fernly Park that evening. Whereas the outhouse is located between the gate and the main house. It would be a convenient place for a meeting.
But who did the stranger come to see? Mrs Ackroyd and Flora are from Canada, so...

I WENT OVER THE EVENING'S EVENTS AGAIN. RALPH HAD ENTERED THROUGH THE WINDOW, OPENED FOR HIM BY ACKROYD. THUS THE REQUEST FOR MONEY AT HALF PAST NINE.

MISS FLORA SAW HER UNCLE ALIVE AT A QUARTER TO TEN. THEREFORE IT MUST BE THE STRANGER WHO MURDERED ACKROYD. HE MAY HAVE BEEN IN LEAGUE WITH PARKER, WHO MAY IN TURN HAVE BEEN BLACKMAILING MRS FERRARS.

Hmm, your little grey cells are working well. But why the telephone call, the moved armchair and the missing forty pounds?

As to the money, Ackroyd must have given it to Ralph.

One more thing is unexplained. Why was Blunt so certain in his own mind that Raymond was with Mr Ackroyd at nine thirty?
And tell me why Ralph has disappeared, my friend...

He had many motives for killing Mr Ackroyd. His inheritance, the stealing of the letter naming him as the blackmailer, his debts...
Three motives, it is almost too much! I am inclined to think, after all, that Ralph is innocent.

THE AFFAIR NOW ENTERED A NEW PHASE. UNTIL THEN I HAD PLAYED WATSON TO POIROT'S SHERLOCK. HENCEFORTH HE NO LONGER TOOK ME INTO HIS CONFIDENCE.
EVERYONE WAS TRYING TO SOLVE THIS PUZZLE. BUT IT WAS POIROT ALONE WHO WAS TO SUCCEED IN FITTING TOGETHER THE PIECES.

MRS ACKROYD SENT FOR ME ON TUESDAY MORNING, WITH SUCH URGENCY THAT I EXPECTED TO FIND HER CLOSE TO DEATH...
I'm prostrated with grief ... prostrated! It's the shock of poor Roger's death...

NONSENSE, I THOUGHT. I WONDERED WHY IT WAS SHE HAD SENT FOR ME?

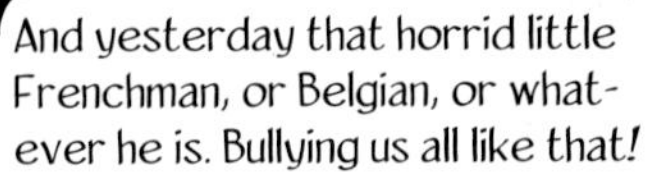
And yesterday that horrid little Frenchman, or Belgian, or whatever he is. Bullying us all like that!

I haven't concealed a thing, from the police or anyone else. It's that girl Ursula Bourne... She wants to make trouble!
MRS ACKROYD IS INCAPABLE OF SPEAKING PLAINLY. I ATTEMPTED TO DISCERN WHAT SHE WAS TRYING TO TELL ME.

IN FACT SHE HAD PLENTY TO HIDE. HOW SHE HAD SUFFERED, SHE SAID! ACKROYD'S MEANNESS... HER MOUNTING DEBTS... HER ATTEMPTS TO BORROW MONEY...
ON FRIDAY AFTERNOON, SHE HAD FOUND THE STUDY EMPTY. PERHAPS SHE COULD TAKE A LOOK AT ACKROYD'S WILL, IN ORDER TO REASSURE HERSELF ABOUT HER FUTURE...?

BUT URSULA BOURNE SURPRISED HER. WHEN ACKROYD RETURNED URSULA ASKED TO SPEAK TO HIM.

That is all?!
Yes...!

At least ... it was I who opened the display case. There were one or two interesting pieces... I thought I would take them to London to be valued.
If they turned out to be valuable, what a delightful surprise it would have been for Roger!

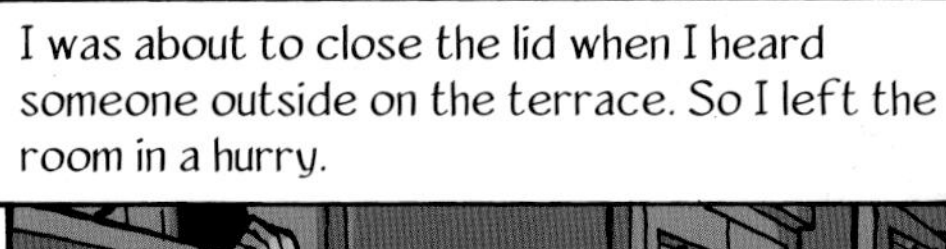
I was about to close the lid when I heard someone outside on the terrace. So I left the room in a hurry.

IT MUST HAVE BEEN MISS RUSSELL, RETURNING FROM THE GARDEN. BUT WHY HAD SHE BEEN THERE?

TAKING MY LEAVE OF MRS ACKROYD, I FOUND URSULA BOURNE IN THE HALL. SHE WAS IN TEARS.

Miss Bourne, I hear that it was you who asked to speak to Mr Ackroyd on Friday.
I meant to leave in any case...

Excuse me, sir, is there any news of Ralph Paton?
No. Do you know where he is...?!

No, truly I don't. Sir, when do they think the murder was done? Before a quarter to ten?

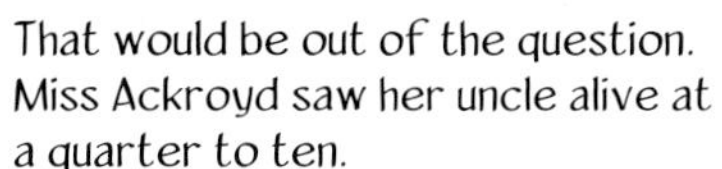
That would be out of the question. Miss Ackroyd saw her uncle alive at a quarter to ten.

WHY THESE TEARS? AND WHY SUCH QUESTIONS?

CAROLINE WAS AT HOME. SHE HAD HAD A VISIT FROM MONSIEUR POIROT.
I am helping him with the case. He wanted me to find out if Ralph's boots were brown or black.
They were brown shoes.

But what connection is there between the colour of Ralph's shoes and Ackroyd's murder?
No James, his boots. I can tell you now...
They were black!

And Mr Raymond has just left. He wanted to see Monsieur Poirot. He'd been to The Larches, but Poirot was out.
IT SEEMED POIROT'S TACTICS WERE AGAIN PROVING TO BE SUCCESSFUL.

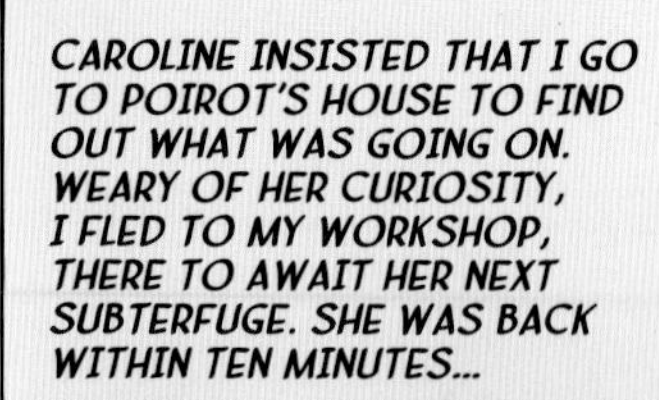
CAROLINE INSISTED THAT I GO TO POIROT'S HOUSE TO FIND OUT WHAT WAS GOING ON. WEARY OF HER CURIOSITY, I FLED TO MY WORKSHOP, THERE TO AWAIT HER NEXT SUBTERFUGE. SHE WAS BACK WITHIN TEN MINUTES...

James, could you take this pot of jam to Monsieur Poirot? Annie's busy. Just leave it on his doorstep.
But if by chance you do see Monsieur Poirot, you might tell him about the boots.

I MADE MY WAY ALMOST AUTOMATICALLY TO POIROT'S HOUSE, WHERE I TOLD HIM ABOUT MY MEETING WITH MRS ACKROYD.

Miss Russell did indeed find the display case open, and she closed it. But why had she been in the garden?

My sister asked me to tell you that Ralph's boots were black and not brown.
She is absolutely positive about this?!

Ah, that is a pity...

May I ask ... when Mrs Russell came to see you in your surgery, what was discussed?
We talked about poisons, and about drugs and drug addiction.

Voilà! An article on drugs, dated Friday. This is what put the idea of cocaine into Miss Russell's head!

How are you, doctor? I was anxious to see you, Monsieur Poirot.

I've a confession to make.
I've been keeping something from you...

I've been badly in debt. But this legacy of 500 pounds has put me back on my feet.
Raglan put the wind up me a little — but I was a fool to worry. Blunt and I were together the whole time the murder was being committed. So I have an alibi.

I'll be off now. Goodbye!

So that's that. Now there's only Blunt who doesn't stand to benefit from Ackroyd's death.
Yes, but the only thing Blunt conceals is his love — and not very well!

Perhaps the murderer and the blackmailer are not the same person?

Very good, doctor! It may be that someone else took the letter — Parker, for example. He may have heard the secret of Mr Ferrars' death from one of his servants and seen the opportunity for blackmail.
Well, I noticed the letter was gone before ... no, *after* Blunt and Raymond arrived. So that widens the field to three — Parker, Blunt and Raymond.

I ACCOMPANIED POIROT TO FERNLY, WHERE HE INTENDED TO TRY A LITTLE EXPERIMENT WITH PARKER.
Mademoiselle Flora, I have some suspicions of Parker. Will you assist me to repeat some of his actions on the night of the crime?

Parker, I want to see if anyone could have heard your conversation with Miss Ackroyd from the terrace, where Major Blunt is waiting.

Reconstruction of the crime, they call it, sir, do they not?
Ah, Parker! You are correct.

35,

Miss had her hand on the doorknob.
I had just closed the door.

Parker?! Mr Ackroyd doesn't wish to be disturbed for the rest of the evening!

Very good, miss. Would you like me to lock up as usual?
Yes, please.

Has your experiment been successful?
Yes, I think so. At any rate, I now know something I wanted to have clarified for me.

WE HELD A LITTLE MAH JONG PARTY, A FINE OPPORTUNITY FOR GOSSIP. AND EACH GUEST HAD A THEORY AS TO THE MURDERER'S IDENTITY...
WAS IT MISS RUSSELL, WITH HER INTEREST IN POISONS? OR MISS ACKROYD, WHO WAS THE LAST TO SEE HER UNCLE ALIVE?

POIROT HAD REMARKED TO CAROLINE ABOUT CRANCHESTER. THIS CLEARLY MEANT RALPH WAS HIDING THERE. AND MISS GANETT HAD SEEN POIROT IN THE TOWN.
CAROLINE ADDED THAT I WASN'T SAYING MUCH. GOADED BY HER, I MENTIONED THE RING FOUND IN THE POND.

THAT MUST MEAN FLORA WAS SECRETLY MARRIED TO RALPH — OR TO RAYMOND. OR PERHAPS ACKROYD TO MRS FERRARS. NO ONE THOUGHT OF FLORA AND BLUNT.
BUT ACCORDING TO CAROLINE, WHO WAS OFTEN RIGHT, FLORA CARED NOTHING FOR RALPH PATON.

THE FUNERALS OF ACKROYD AND MRS FERRARS WERE HELD THE NEXT DAY.
My friend, you must help me to question Parker. He should await us at my house at this very minute. He is the blackmailer, or... I hope it is he!

Good morning, sir.
Good morning, Parker. *Mon ami*, have you made many attempts at blackmail? And please don't wear that air of an injured man! Why were you so anxious to overhear the conversation in Mr Ackroyd's study on the night of the crime?

I wasn't...!
Your last master, Major Ellerby, he was addicted to drugs, was he not? And he had committed a crime while he was abroad.

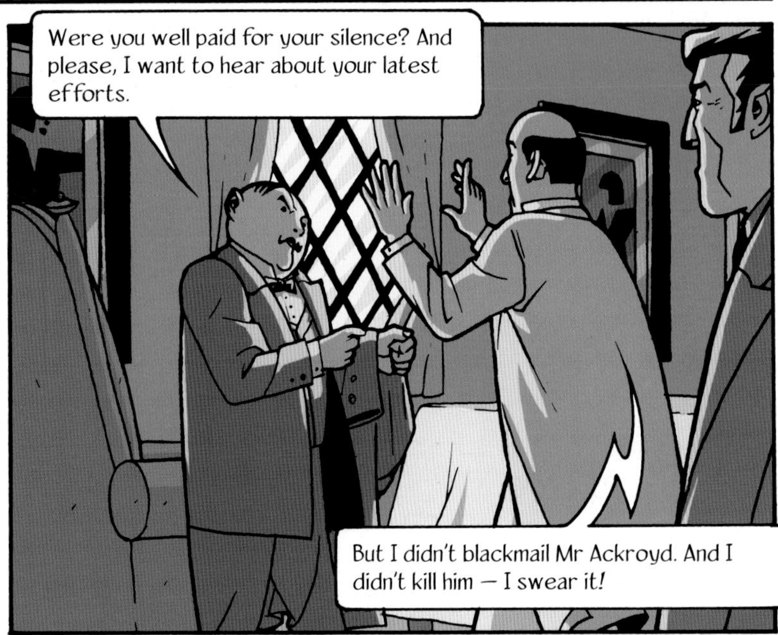
Were you well paid for your silence? And please, I want to hear about your latest efforts.
But I didn't blackmail Mr Ackroyd. And I didn't kill him — I swear it!

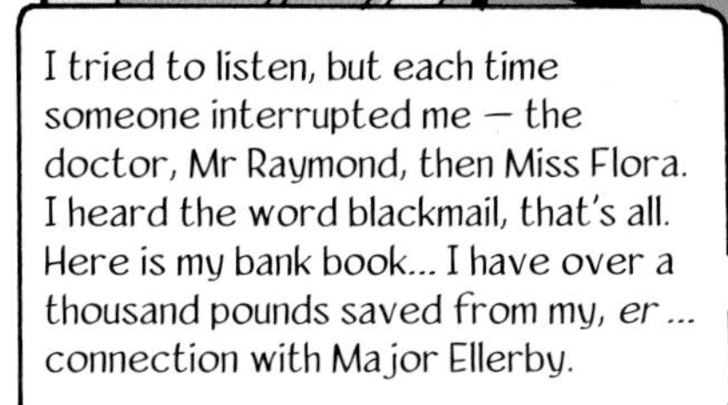
I tried to listen, but each time someone interrupted me — the doctor, Mr Raymond, then Miss Flora. I heard the word blackmail, that's all. Here is my bank book... I have over a thousand pounds saved from my, *er* ... connection with Major Ellerby.

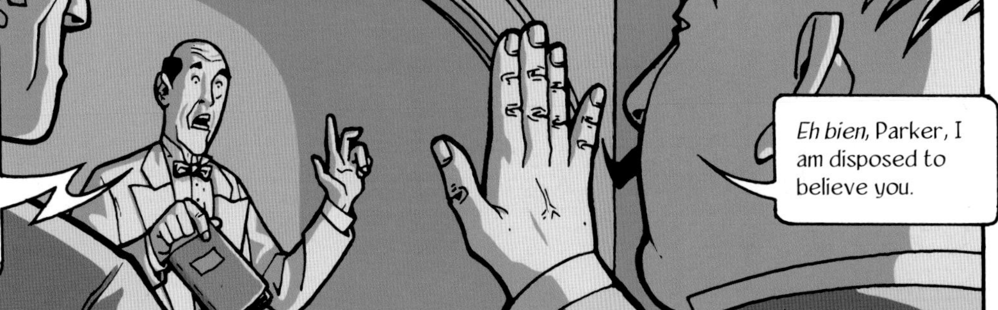
Eh bien, Parker, I am disposed to believe you.

Parker genuinely believes Mr Ackroyd was being blackmailed. He knows nothing of Mrs Ferrars. But let us visit Mr Hammond, so as to clear Parker completely, or...

I apologize. I fall into the bad habit of leaving my sentences unfinished!

I've got a confession to make ... I left out something about that ring you found in the pond.
Ah! It is no matter. The explanation, it was simple.

WE MADE OUR WAY TO HAMMOND'S, WHERE I TOLD THE LAWYER ABOUT MY DISCUSSION WITH ACKROYD ON THE NIGHT OF THE CRIME.
Monsieur, you acted for the late Mrs Ferrars. Are you able to tell us the amount she paid to her blackmailer?
Twenty thousand.

Twenty thousand pounds?!!!
Mrs Ferrars was a wealthy woman, doctor.

Having gained such a huge sum, Parker wouldn't have continued being a butler...
While Raymond's debts were just five hundred pounds. As to Blunt...

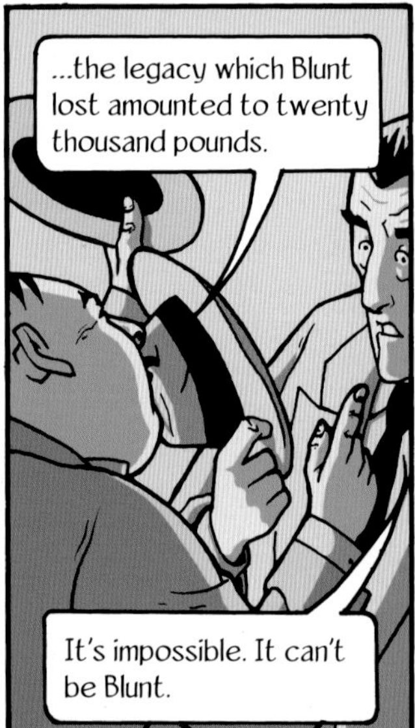
...the legacy which Blunt lost amounted to twenty thousand pounds.
It's impossible. It can't be Blunt.

But as for the blue letter, there is another possibility...
Ackroyd himself may have burnt it after you left him.

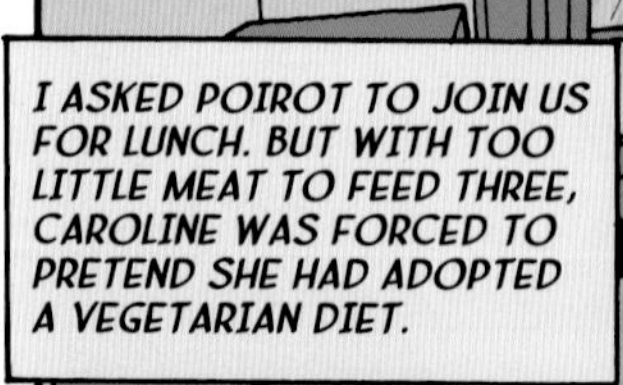
I ASKED POIROT TO JOIN US FOR LUNCH. BUT WITH TOO LITTLE MEAT TO FEED THREE, CAROLINE WAS FORCED TO PRETEND SHE HAD ADOPTED A VEGETARIAN DIET.

ASKING WHETHER RALPH HAD BEEN FOUND IN CRANCHESTER, SHE WAS SURPRISED TO HEAR THAT POIROT HAD BEEN THERE ONLY TO VISIT THE DENTIST. CHANGING THE SUBJECT, SHE SPECULATED ON WHAT MIGHT HAVE BEEN MY FATE WITHOUT HER TO LOOK AFTER ME.

SHE THEN REGALED US WITH HER OPINIONS ON THE MURDER. ALL THE SUSPECTS HAD ALIBIS EXCEPT RALPH AND FLORA. AND SHE HAD KNOWN RALPH SINCE HE WAS A CHILD...

FLORA, HOWEVER, COULD HAVE KILLED ACKROYD BEFORE MEETING PARKER. THE BUTLER HAD NOT HEARD HER SAY GOODNIGHT TO HER UNCLE ... BUT I AM CERTAIN SHE'S NO KILLER.

Let us take an ordinary man. In need of money, he stumbles on an acquaintance's secret.
His first impulse is to reveal his knowledge — but then he sees the chance of money. And blackmail!

But he must have more and more money... Finally, his victim commits suicide. But not before, in desperation, speaking out. Exposed, the blackmailer takes a dagger and strikes. Afterwards he will be himself once more ... but if the need arises, again he will strike.
You mean Ralph Paton? You have no business to condemn him like that!

TRING!!

Poirot! They've arrested a man in Liverpool. His name is Charles Kent. They think he's the stranger I saw at the gate!

ACCOMPANIED BY RAGLAN, POIROT AND I LEFT STRAIGHT AWAY TO IDENTIFY CHARLES KENT.
Monsieur Poirot, you were quite right about the fingerprints on the dagger. They were Mr Ackroyd's own!

Are you Dr Sheppard, sir? The suspect admits that he was in King's Abbot that Friday.
And Monsieur Poirot ... Can you tell us where Ralph Paton is hiding?

It would not be wise at this moment.
I HAD TO BITE MY LIP TO PREVENT MYSELF FROM LAUGHING.

It's him all right. I recognize his voice.
Recognize my voice? Where from?!

You were outside the gates of Fernly Park on Friday evening.
39,

Yeah, I heard an old fellow was done in that evening. Trying to pin it on me, are you? I went to Fernly to meet someone. Left at twenty-five past nine.
You can ask at the Dog and Whistle. It's a mile from Fernly. I kicked up a bit of a row there. Quarter to ten, it was.

Where were you born, Mr Kent?
I'm pure English, me...

Yes ... born in the county of Kent, I fancy. Under certain circumstances, a man born in Kent may bear that very name.
I THOUGHT CHARLES KENT WAS ABOUT TO SPRING AT POIROT. RAGLAN WAS CONFIDENT HE HAD HIS BLACKMAILER.

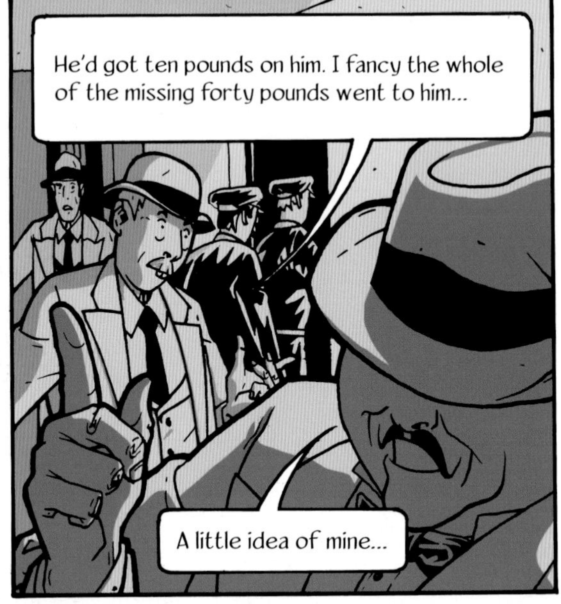
He'd got ten pounds on him. I fancy the whole of the missing forty pounds went to him...
A little idea of mine...

AS I NOW KNOW, POIROT HAD ALREADY SOLVED THE PUZZLE. THE FOLLOWING MORNING I MET RAGLAN.
Charles Kent's alibi is genuine. The barmaid at the Dog and Whistle remembers him all right.

Poirot claims that the reason Kent went to Fernly is because he was born in Kent!
Ha! Ha! Monsieur Poirot and his fanciful ideas!. Runs in the family. His nephew is quite off his rocker!

THE INFORMATION HAD COME FROM CAROLINE. I HAVE NEVER BEEN ABLE TO TEACH HER TO KEEP A FAMILY SECRET.
WE SET OFF TO VISIT THE BELGIAN MADMAN.

POIROT RECOMMENDED THAT KENT SHOULD NOT BE RELEASED.
Do you remember, Parker saw Miss Ackroyd outside her uncle's study? He did not see her come out of the room.

PERHAPS SHE HAD BEEN ON THE STAIRS LEADING TO MR ACKROYD'S BEDROOM. SHE HAD STOLEN THE MONEY TO SETTLE SOME SMALL DEBT. BUT HALFWAY DOWN SHE HEARD PARKER IN THE HALLWAY.
IN ORDER TO AVOID SUSPICION SHE PRETENDED TO HAVE COME OUT OF THE STUDY. SHE REPEATED THE ORDER THAT MR ACKROYD WAS NOT TO BE DISTURBED, AND THEN WENT UPSTAIRS TO HER OWN ROOM.

WHEN THE POLICE CAME, SHE THOUGHT THE THEFT HAD BEEN DISCOVERED. SHE STUCK TO HER STORY, BUT WHEN SHE HEARD THAT HER UNCLE WAS DEAD, SHE FELL INTO A FAINT.

But you told me the reconstruction was to test Parker!
Everybody has something to hide, *mon cher docteur*.

SO WE MADE OUR WAY TO FERNLY TO SPEAK WITH MISS ACKROYD.

Monsieur Poirot is right. I stole the money ... I've run up so many debts, promised to pay them... Ralph and I are both weak... But I'm not an innocent, simple little girl, Major Blunt...
If by confessing I could have cleared Ralph's name, I would have done it!

Ralph! Always Ralph!
You don't understand, you never will!

Inspector Raglan, the forty pounds was given to me by Mr Ackroyd.
Miss Flora never touched it!

It is very good, what you have just done.
Mademoiselle Flora only agreed to marry Ralph to please her uncle — and to escape her life here.

My sister told me something very similar. And she's always right about these things.
Your feelings for Mademoiselle Flora — you must declare them! But perhaps this matter...
No, poor Flora ... she got in a mess with money and didn't dare tell her uncle. Poor girl...

This alters everything, this does. So Miss Ackroyd didn't see her uncle...
We'll have to go over the alibis again from nine thirty onwards.

If Kent spoke to Ackroyd at half past nine, he could have killed him and got to the Dog and Whistle by a quarter to ten. But he couldn't also have been at the station to make that telephone call.

We always come up against that telephone call!

Ralph Paton might have found his uncle murdered... He got the wind up and cleared off. But then thought Ackroyd might still be alive and called the doctor...

HAVING TAKEN LEAVE OF POIROT AND RAGLAN, I ATTENDED TO MY PATIENTS. AFTERWARDS I WENT TO MY WORKSHOP. IT'S A PLACE CAROLINE HATES, BECAUSE THE MAID IS ALLOWED NOWHERE NEAR IT.

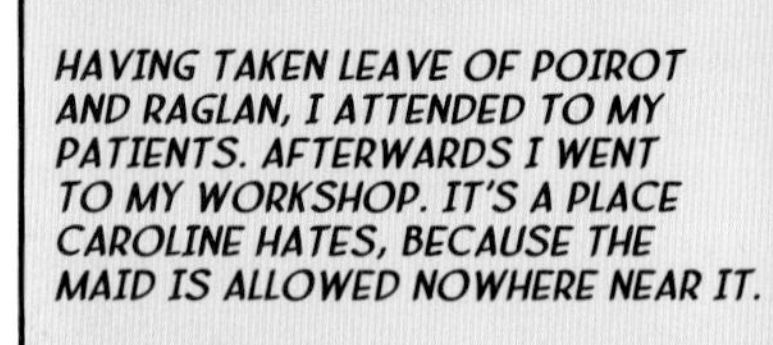

WHILE I WAS ENGAGED IN REPAIRING AN ALARM CLOCK, CAROLINE APPEARED IN ORDER TO ANNOUNCE POIROT'S ARRIVAL.

Ah, doctor, I come to tell you that you have still one patient to see. It is a lady with whom I wish much to speak.

Miss Russell!
I must say, concerning the matter of Mademoiselle Flora, that the inspector was surprised. But you weren't...

I had a feeling about it.
Indeed so ... and I profited by the inspector's discomfiture to induce him to grant me a little favour...

AT POIROT'S REQUEST, AN ITEM HAD BEEN PRINTED IN THE NEWSPAPER REPORTING RALPH'S ARREST WHILE EMBARKING FOR AMERICA.
But it isn't true!
Ralph is not in Liverpool!
Indeed he is not in Liverpool. Come now, use your little grey cells!

POIROT DISPLAYED SOME INTEREST IN MY WIRELESS SET, SO I SHOWED HIM ONE OR TWO OF MY LITTLE INVENTIONS. THEN THE BELL RANG ANNOUNCING MY PATIENT.

Good morning, Mademoiselle Russell.You know Charles Kent has been arrested in Liverpool?
What of it? Who is this Charles Kent?
FINALLY, IT CAME TO ME. HER VOICE WAS THAT OF CHARLES KENT!

Mademoiselle Flora lied to us. Ackroyd died before a quarter to ten. Charles Kent was present at that time, so it would seem he was the man responsible.
Miss Flora...? But...
He came to see me! I beg you to believe me!
Charles Kent is my son!
I was young ... it was long ago, down in Kent. I was not married... He never knew I was his mother.

He turned out badly — took to drink, then drugs. I paid his passage to Canada. Somehow he found out there that I was his mother.
He wrote asking for money. Finally he informed me that he was back in this country.

I WENT TO SEE DR SHEPPARD, HOPING HIS ADDICTION MIGHT BE CURED. I SENT HIM A MESSAGE SAYING I WOULD MEET HIM IN THE OUTHOUSE. I TOOK ALL THE MONEY I HAD, AND HE LEFT AT TWENTY-FIVE PAST NINE, HEADING FOR THE GATE.
WHEN I WENT BACK TO THE HOUSE, MAJOR BLUNT WAS ON THE TERRACE. SO AS TO AVOID HIM, I WENT INTO THE HOUSE THROUGH THE DRAWING ROOM.

43,

Ought I... ought I to tell all this to Inspector Raglan?
It may come to that. But let us not be hasty. The man to whom Ackroyd was talking cannot be your son. All will yet be well.

Thank you, Monsieur Poirot. You do believe Charles is innocent, don't you?

We always come back to Ralph Paton. How did you spot that it was Miss Russell whom Kent came to meet?
As soon as we found that feather. It suggested drugs, and I remembered her questions to you ... then the newspaper article. It all seemed clear.

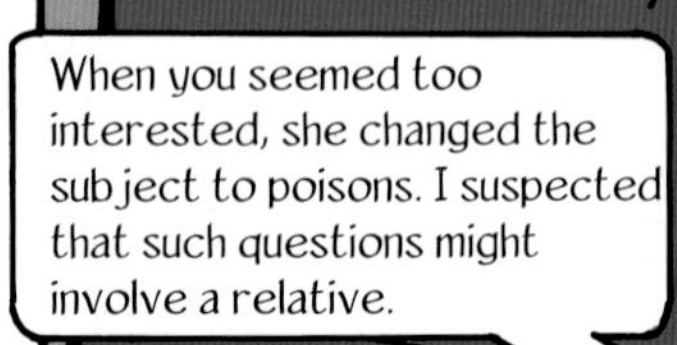
When you seemed too interested, she changed the subject to poisons. I suspected that such questions might involve a relative.
I SUGGESTED THAT POIROT STAYED TO LUNCH. BUT HE DECLINED, SAYING HE DID NOT WISH TO FORCE CAROLINE TO BECOME VEGETARIAN FOR A SECOND DAY. NOT MUCH ESCAPES HERCULE POIROT.

THE PARAGRAPH INSERTED BY POIROT ALSO APPEARED IN THE NEXT MORNING'S NEWSPAPER.
You must stop Ralph being hanged. Declare him not mentally responsible! I believe the patients are very happy in Broadmoor...
CAROLINE'S WORDS REMINDED ME OF SOMETHING.

I never knew that Poirot had a mad nephew.
It's a great grief to his family. They're afraid he'll have to go into an institution.

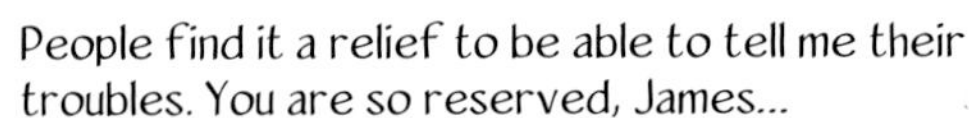
People find it a relief to be able to tell me their troubles. You are so reserved, James...

But I am always discreet. For instance, I shouldn't dream of asking Poirot who it was who arrived at his house early this morning!

HOWEVER, CAROLINE MADE FULL USE OF HER DISCRETION IN TRYING TO DISCOVER FROM POIROT HIS GUEST'S IDENTITY.

LATER POIROT TOOK ME FOR A WALK IN THE DIRECTION OF FERNLY PARK...
This evening, at my house, I desire to have a little conference with those who live at Fernly. And with you yourself, of course.
You will invite them, yes? If I go they will demand what my idea is. I will promenade myself in the grounds!

MRS ACKROYD WAS AT HOME. SHE HAD NEWS – MISS ACKROYD WAS ENGAGED TO BLUNT. FINALLY I WAS ABLE TO GIVE HER POIROT'S MESSAGE.

I THEN JOINED POIROT, GASPING FOR BREATH, AT THE GATE OF FERNLY PARK.

ON OUR RETURN HOME, WE FOUND CAROLINE AWAITING US WITH THE NEWS THAT URSULA BOURNE WAS IN THE DINING ROOM.
Ah, Ursula Bourne ... or is it rather Ursula Paton? Mrs Ralph Paton. Have you by chance lost a ring?

The paper says Ralph has been arrested in Liverpool. So I need not pretend any longer. I'll tell you the whole story.
My family was ruined when my father died. My sister married Richard Folliott, and I decided to earn a living as a maid. So my sister gave me a reference...
SHE AND RALPH FELL IN LOVE AND WERE MARRIED IN SECRET. BUT ACKROYD WISHED RALPH TO MARRY FLORA, AND RALPH COULD NOT RESIST THE CHANCE TO CLEAR HIS SUBSTANTIAL DEBTS.

SO AS TO CONCEAL IT FROM URSULA, RALPH ASKED THAT HIS ENGAGEMENT TO FLORA SHOULD BE KEPT SECRET.

BUT ACKROYD NEVERTHELESS ANNOUNCED IT. URSULA MET RALPH IN THE WOODS TO TELL HIM SHE WOULD INFORM ACKROYD OF THE TRUTH.

ACKROYD WAS ANGRY WITH BOTH HUSBAND AND WIFE. THEY MET THAT EVENING IN THE OUTHOUSE, WHERE EACH REPROACHED THE OTHER BITTERLY. URSULA'S APRON WAS TORN.
45.

Everything points to Ralph as the murderer... Mr Ackroyd would have disinherited him. I had to keep quiet. I left Ralph in the outhouse at twenty-five to ten and was in my room by a quarter to ten. I haven't seen him since.
Don't worry about Ralph. Newspapers do not always print the truth.

Can anyone prove that you were in your room from a quarter to ten?
No, but... *Oh!* They might think I was the murderer!

I do not believe so. But as for Ralph...
Perhaps he thought I had done it ... and he ran away to divert suspicion. Dr Sheppard, Ralph considered you his best friend in the village. You don't know where he is?

No.
That is true enough. But one thing I should like to know... Was Ralpf wearing shoes or boots on the night of the crime?

I don't remember.
A pity! But don't torment yourself. Please take some rest ... I should like you to attend my little reunion this evening.

Ah, I miss *mon ami* Hastings — always when I had a big case, he was so helpful. And he always kept a record of such cases..
I've, *er,* tried my hand at writing some notes.

Merveilleux! Let me see it, this instant!
Certainly ... it's just that ...

Sometimes you have referred to me as comic — perhaps even ridiculous? Me, I have the mind above such trifles.
SOMEWHAT DOUBTFUL, I GAVE HIM MY MANUSCRIPT. BY NOW I WAS DUE AT MY SURGERY, SO I LEFT POIROT TO READ IT.
46.

LATER THAT EVENING I FOUND POIROT IN MY WORKSHOP.
You are too modest! A very meticulous account. It has helped me considerably.
Now we must go and set the stage for my little performance. Finally you will appreciate Hercule Poirot at his true worth!

Caroline, I must ask you to remain here. Among our company will be a murderer!

ONCE THE ROOM WAS READY, THE PARTY FROM FERNLY TOOK THEIR SEATS.
Allow me to introduce Mrs Ralph Paton.

Ralph! Married to Bourne?
I am ... very glad for you both!

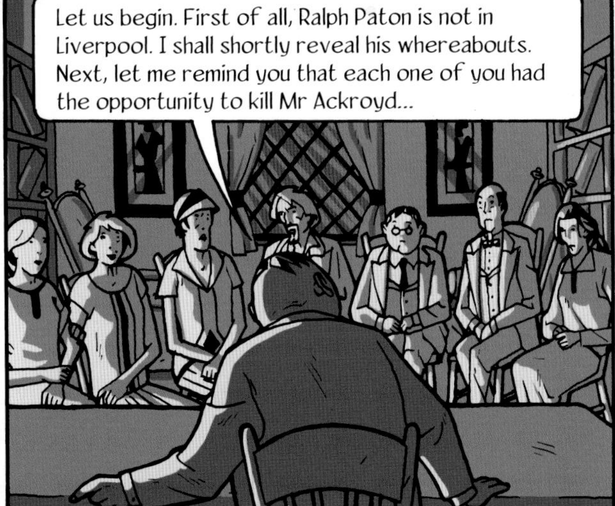
Let us begin. First of all, Ralph Paton is not in Liverpool. I shall shortly reveal his whereabouts. Next, let me remind you that each one of you had the opportunity to kill Mr Ackroyd...

The solution to the puzzle lies in the answer to the question: to whom was Mr Ackroyd talking at nine thirty?

But at nine thirty Ralph and Ursula Bourne were in the outhouse.
Charles Kent had already left.

In fact, was anyone with Mr Ackroyd at all?
But I definitely heard him talking to someone. And not just me — so did Blunt.

Blunt believed Mr Ackroyd was talking to you. "The calls on my funds ... impossible to accede..." The kind of phrases one would use when dictating a letter.

Now, no other voice than Ackroyd's was heard. I have discovered that he secretly purchased a dictaphone from the young man who called on Wednesday.
He must have meant to surprise me — he was fond of such tricks! He was probably playing with it like a new toy.

It explains why Blunt thought you were in the study. To whom else would he dictate a letter?
At the same time Blunt glimpsed the figure of Ursula Bourne, on her way to the outhouse, dressed in her white apron.

So that still leaves Mr Ackroyd alive at half past nine. And only Ralph Paton ... if only he would come forward...!
I know where Ralph is hiding.

In Cranchester?

Always this idea of Cranchester!

No! He is — here! Doctor, you alone kept your secret from me. But all along I have had my suspicions.

SUDDENLY I FELT UNWELL.

You went to the Three Boars on the night of the murder to find Ralph. He was not there, but you met him on your way home.
Yes, I admit it ... When I saw Ralph that afternoon, he told me everything. That night I warned him that he might be forced to incriminate his wife by giving evidence...

With Dr Sheppard's help, I decided to disappear.
It must be somewhere near at hand ... somewhere isolated, quiet. *Ah yes!* A nursing home, a clinic for the mentally unwell...

I invented a nephew who is mentally disturbed and ask of Mademoiselle Sheppard some suitable homes. She gave me the names of two close by.
Her brother had sent patients to both... and in one of them I found Ralph Paton.

Dr Sheppard has stood by me and done what he thought best. But I see now that I should have come forward to face the music!
Anyway, you know most of it... I left the outhouse about nine forty-five and tramped about trying to think. But I have no alibi.

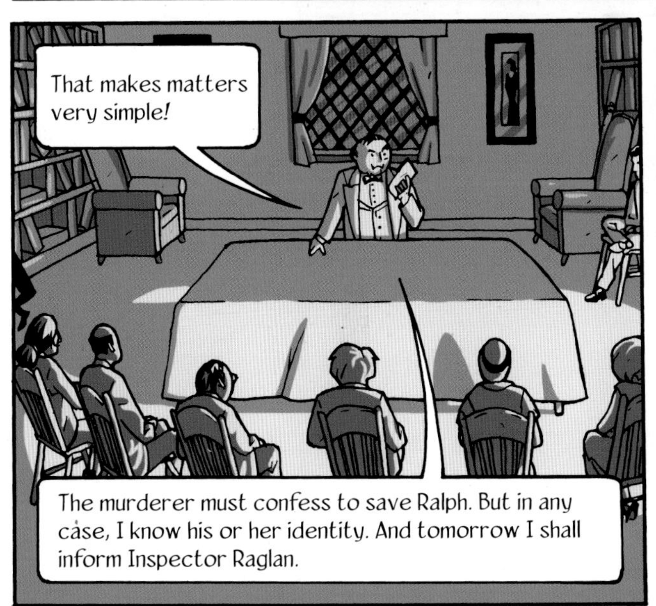
That makes matters very simple!
The murderer must confess to save Ralph. But in any case, I know his or her identity. And tomorrow I shall inform Inspector Raglan.

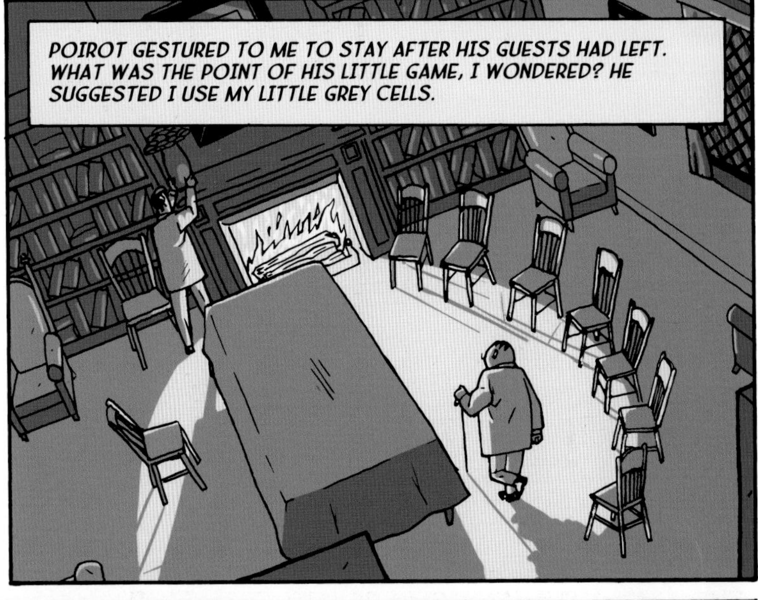
POIROT GESTURED TO ME TO STAY AFTER HIS GUESTS HAD LEFT. WHAT WAS THE POINT OF HIS LITTLE GAME, I WONDERED? HE SUGGESTED I USE MY LITTLE GREY CELLS.

Were you trying to force a confession from the murderer? Or perhaps make him reveal himself by attempting to silence you?
I am not sufficiently heroic for that. But the culprit cannot escape. There is only one way out...

Consider the telephone call... If Ralph were guilty, he would not have made it. Nor could anyone in the house.
So there must have been an accomplice. But why was the call made?

It was made to ensure that the crime was discovered that same evening. Thus the murderer could ensure his presence as soon as the door was opened!
Suppose the murderer wanted to remove some item from the room — something placed on the table near the window and therefore hidden by the armchair which had been moved?

The murderer needed to be on the spot to remove this item. Only Major Blunt, Mr Raymond, Parker and yourself were there...
...and Parker, living at Fernly Park, could be on the scene at any time.

Now, what was this object which must be recovered?

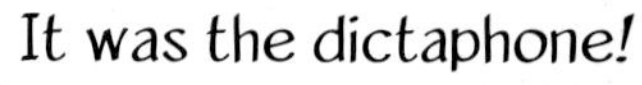
It was the dictaphone!

Now, a dictaphone records the voice — and also repeats it!

At nine thirty Mr Ackroyd was dead. It was the dictaphone speaking, not the man.
And the murderer switched it on. So he was in the room at that minute?

No! Perhaps the murderer employed some mechanical device ... even an alarm clock...
...a device requiring a certain knowledge of mechanics.

At the Three Boars the police found one pair of Ralph's shoes. He wore a second pair...

But did he also have a pair of boots, which the murderer could have stolen? I asked your sister to find out about the colour...
...in order to disguise my need to confirm that Ralph indeed had a pair!

Mademoiselle Flora did not see the dagger in the display case that evening...
...because the murderer had already taken it!

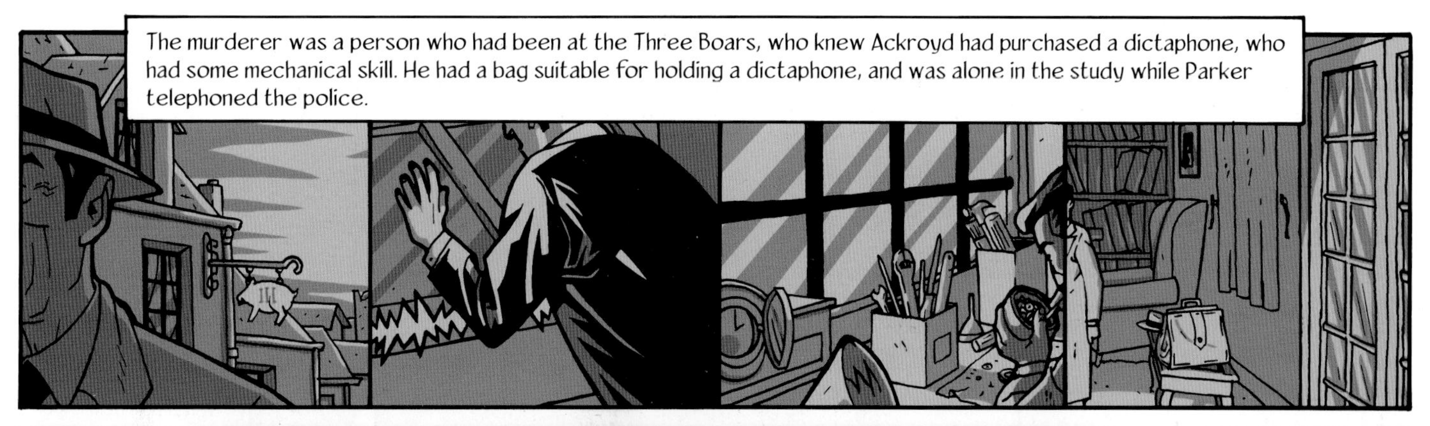
The murderer was a person who had been at the Three Boars, who knew Ackroyd had purchased a dictaphone, who had some mechanical skill. He had a bag suitable for holding a dictaphone, and was alone in the study while Parker telephoned the police.

It was you, Dr Sheppard!
It takes five minutes to walk from the house at Fernly to the gate. Yet, that night, you left the house at ten to nine, but reached the gate only at nine.

You killed Ackroyd and left the room, telling Parker he was not to be disturbed. You went to the outhouse, where you put on Ralph's boots.
You returned to the study through the window, which you yourself had left open, in order to lock the door from inside.

Your footprints incriminated Ralph, while the locked door prevented anyone from entering.
You returned home to your sister, while at half past nine the dictaphone started to replay Ackroyd's voice. A perfect alibi!

You're mad! *Why would I murder Ackroyd?*
Who else, doctor, could have known that Mrs Ferrars poisoned her husband? You blackmailed her. You invented a legacy to account for the money you obtained from Mrs Ferrars and gambled away.

A steward from the liner *Orion* came to your surgery that evening before departing for Liverpool.
ORION
He has cabled me explaining how you asked him to take a note to a patient. He was to call you from the station with the reply — which was "*No answer.*" So the telephone call was genuine. Your sister saw you take it. But you alone knew what in fact was said — nothing!

Please, doctor, Ralph Paton must be cleared! Finish your manuscript — by telling the whole story.
For the sake of your good sister, I am willing to allow you a way out...

IT IS FIVE IN THE MORNING. I AM VERY TIRED — BUT MY STORY IS FINISHED.
A STRANGE END TO MY MANUSCRIPT ... I MEANT IT TO BE THE HISTORY OF ONE OF POIROT'S FAILURES. ODD HOW THINGS PAN OUT.

POOR ACKROYD ... I GAVE HIM A CHANCE TO READ THAT LETTER — AT LEAST, KNOWING HOW STUBBORN HE WAS, I GAVE HIM THE CHANCE NOT TO READ IT.
HE HAD GIVEN ME THE DICTAPHONE TO REPAIR, AND MY DOCTOR'S BAG PROVED VERY USEFUL FOR RETURNING IT THAT EVENING.

THEN, IN THE TEN MINUTES AFTER THE LETTER ARRIVED ... PERHAPS I INTENDED TO KILL HIM ALL ALONG, CONVINCED MRS FERRARS WOULD HAVE TOLD HIM EVERYTHING. NOW ALL WAS IN PLACE. THE DICTAPHONE ON THE TABLE, THE CHAIR MOVED TO HIDE IT...
I SHOULD HAVE KNOWN THAT PARKER, WITH HIS TRAINED SERVANT'S EYE, WOULD NOTICE THE ARMCHAIR. THEN FLORA CONFUSED MATTERS BY SAYING SHE HAD SEEN HER UNCLE ALIVE. AND MOST OF ALL, I FEARED MY SISTER CAROLINE WOULD GUESS...

BUT FOR ONCE, SHE'LL NEVER KNOW THE TRUTH.
POIROT AND RAGLAN WILL KEEP THE STORY QUIET. AND MY MANUSCRIPT WILL CLEAR RALPH...

CAROLINE WILL GRIEVE FOR ME, BUT GRIEF PASSES...
CAROLINE...

I SHALL CHOOSE VERONAL TO POISON MYSELF. A KIND OF POETIC JUSTICE.
NOT THAT I PITY MRS FERRARS. NOR DO I PITY MYSELF.

52,

THE STORY HAS COME FULL CIRCLE.

BUT HOW I WISH HERCULE POIROT HAD RETIRED ELSEWHERE TO GROW VEGETABLE MARROWS.

à ma mère

AGATHA CHRISTIE (1890–1976) is known throughout the world as *The Queen of Crime*. Her first book, *The Mysterious Affair at Styles*, was written during the First World War and introduced us to Hercule Poirot, the Belgian detective with the "Little Grey Cells", who was destined to reappear in nearly 100 different adventures over the next 50 years. Agatha also created the elderly crime-solver, Miss Marple, as well as more than 2,000 colourful characters across her 80 crime novels and short story collections. Agatha Christie's books have sold over one billion copies in the English language and another billion in more than 100 countries, making her the best-selling novelist in history. Now, following years of successful adaptations including stage, films, television, radio, audiobooks and computer games, some of her most famous novels, starting with *Murder on the Orient Express*, *Death on the Nile*, *The Murder on the Links* and *The Secret of Chimneys*, have been adapted into comic strips so that they may be enjoyed by yet another generation of readers.